Praise for
THE BOOK OF THE UNKNOWN

"Echoes of Isaac Bashevis Singer, Sholom Aleichem and S. Y. Agnon sound throughout this high-concept collection's engaging stories.... Unusual and charming stories that successfully revive a nearly forgotten form of storytelling. One hopes we will hear more of these Lamedh-Vov and their all-too-human struggles and triumphs."
— *Kirkus Reviews*

"[Keats's] allegorical world resembles some hybrid of Robin Hood's Sherwood Forest and Shrek's moss-covered environs. Visions of cloaks and pushcarts and thatched roofs abound throughout each wonderful fable as it weaves together mysticism and conflict.... Keats's characters occupy a world where goodness prevails and redemption finds the right person.... This is not our world, but it is most definitely one worth reading."
— *Booklist*

"Celebrated conceptual artist Keats returns with brilliant dexterity to the traditional medium of words for his latest offering: a warm and gentle collection of folktales about the intersection between mysticism and magic and the simple verity of human virtue. A contemporary addition to the rich canon of Jewish folklore, *The Book of the Unknown* reminds us why fairy tales never die, especially when they can be so skillfully redefined by modern-day masters of the form."
— MARK DUNN, author of *Ella Minnow Pea*

THE BOOK OF THE UNKNOWN

THE BOOK
OF THE
UNKNOWN

Tales of the Thirty-six

JONATHON KEATS

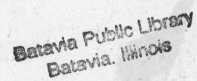

RANDOM HOUSE TRADE PAPERBACKS

NEW YORK

A Random House Trade Paperback Original

Copyright © 2009 by Jonathon Keats

Published in the United States by Random House Trade Paperbacks,
an imprint of The Random House Publishing Group,
a division of Random House, Inc., New York.

RANDOM HOUSE and colophon are registered trademarks of
Random House, Inc.

LIBRARY OF CONGRESS CATALOGING-IN-PUBLICATION DATA

Keats, Jonathon.
The book of the unknown: tales of the thirty-six/Jonathon Keats.
p.   cm.
ISBN 978-0-8129-7897-1
1. Jews—Fiction.   2. Antiheroes—Fiction.   3. Fables.   I. Title.
PS3561.E2526B66 2009
813'.54—dc22   2008016562

Printed in the United States of America

www.randomhouse.com

9 8 7 6 5 4 3 2 1

Book design by Carole Lowenstein

Despise no man and deem nothing impossible,
for every man has his hour and every thing its place.

—TALMUD

CONTENTS

THE BOOK OF THE UNKNOWN

AUTHOR'S FOREWORD

Destiny is an accident.

Twenty-three years ago, while I was in graduate school, the stone remains of a lost synagogue were discovered by construction workers in a small German town. The laborers were digging the foundation for an apartment complex, and the landowner, heavily in debt, permitted building to stop for just one week while every Jewish student in the region was dispatched to save all that could be preserved.

There, beneath a scattering of rocks, I found the documents that would make my career, a crypt of interred contracts and commentaries and correspondence, buried beneath the temple because religious law forbade the destruction of any scrap of paper bearing the name of God. From that textual cemetery, or *genizah,* I resurrected the traditions and rituals of an extinct Jewish village. The dissertation I wrote established my reputation. By my thirtieth birthday, I'd become a leading scholar in my field, lecturing around the world. The only son of immigrants, shtetl peasants who'd escaped the Holocaust, I was living the life that my parents had struggled to bequeath, the embodiment of their dreams.

My mother died in 1998, and my father followed her in 2004. By then my books about lost Jewish communities and their hidden rituals were standard texts. I blush to confess that footnotes from my dissertation had become subdisciplines, complete with postdocs and conference sessions. I cringe to admit that my name was cited in papers concerning archeological offal that would have passed as landfill when I was in school. Even as interest in shtetl life expanded, material dwindled. The field was drifting from the scholarly to the frivolous, and I was, to my chagrin, the honored paterfamilias. As I slouched into middle age, acquiring my father's paunch, I was settling into academic complacence.

It did not have to be that way. That's the shame of it. For nearly a quarter century, I'd retained a secret, holding on to a discovery I'd made while excavating that German *genizah,* preserving a fragment that, if my suspicion was right, would eclipse all that I'd yet achieved. Until my father's death, I'd carefully concealed the fragment, and suppressed the suspicion. I had avoided the whole subject because it was so improbable, completely implausible to anyone who wasn't superstitious.

And yet, for all my sober professionalism, I'd never quite dismissed it. Superstition had saved my family. My father had been a deeply superstitious man who'd believed that the years of pogroms could be read in the Sabbath flame, an ancient tradition in his native village. The Nazis had invaded in the year he foretold, and the genocide had begun within months of my parents' arrival on Ellis Island, the town's only survivors.

My father never forgot. Rather than assimilate, he carried the old country within him. He taught me the ways of dybbuks, and showed me how to make sacred amulets. He told me of powerful seraphim unmentioned in Torah. If I paid close attention, he rewarded me with honey cakes. But if I asked too many questions, inquiring about the anatomy of angels or the motivations of demons, he responded with strange tales about a rogue Kabbalist whose curiosity had once unmoored the world.

The Kabbalist was named Yaakov ben Eleazer, and, as I later learned, his legend had many versions. According to some, he'd been a prodigy, an orphan whose only yeshiva companions were books with which he held deep discussions on subjects that fellow students could not find when they read the same passages. He memorized the Babylonian Talmud, that great compendium of law and lore, before the beard grew on his chin. Forbidden to study Kabbalah because of his age, he conjured his own version, too arcane for even the rabbis to fathom. Or maybe not. Other stories claimed that he stole sacred Kabbalistic texts from the synagogue library, yet misunderstood them so totally that he rendered them incomprehensible to learned men. By this reckoning, he was not a prodigy scholar but a precocious charlatan.

What nobody disputes is that Yaakov could sing. After his voice broke, mothers kept their daughters well covered in synagogue, wrapped up in mantles and shawls, lest his baritone open wombs and his words gestate children. The women's concerns were unwarranted. Yaakov wasn't training his voice for matinee seduction. He had studied that God sang the world into existence using the sounds of the Hebrew alphabet, and that those syllables, rightly pronounced, were all powerful. The orphan, lacking every earthly influence, intended to produce that heavenly music in his gullet.

For a time, he must have kept his ambitions sotto voce, as we hear about him again only as a grown man, assistant to the cantor at the synagogue. He kept a small room in the temple attic. Strange noises emanated from that cell at night. Scholars in the adjacent study house claimed they sounded less like prayer than copulation with demons.

Yaakov responded to their accusations by revealing the system that he'd been developing since summoning Kabbalah as a child. He believed that the true sounds of the Hebrew alphabet were concealed between the consonants, where ordinary people put vowels. Those vowels, never written in ancient days, muffled the music that carried God's word. He wouldn't explain how to read the music, but, compelled to prove his system, promised to betray a great secret: With the unearthly power his song gave him, he would discover the thirty-six hallowed names of the Lamedh-Vov.

Or was this all rumor? Had others simply heard unnatural sounds and assumed that the orphan who'd once conjured, or stolen, Kabbalah was pursuing greater dangers? Either way, the secret of the Lamedh-Vov, the notion that it might be revealed, would have terrified as much as it beguiled.

The Hebrew letters Lamedh and Vov together signify the number thirty-six. That many righteous people are needed at any time, Talmud relates, to justify humanity in the mind of God. Without them, the world would be doomed. Yet, unlike the elect of other religions, these living saints—I use the word *saint* because no other term in the English language adequately conveys their spiritually elevated status—are necessarily anonymous. Learn the identity of a Lamedh-Vov, and that person would no longer be among the thirty-six; another righteous man or woman somewhere would be called for to keep the world in balance. Why the secrecy? Why are the elect themselves even forbidden from knowing their virtue? The self-righteous are abundant in any time. The saintly are of another order.

By seeking to learn the thirty-six names, then, Yaakov ben Eleazer was putting the world in jeopardy. The Lamedh-Vov have been described as pillars, replaced one at a time on account of death or other events. But to grasp for the entire roster? Yaakov would fell every pillar at once.

Legend claims that he did it. Late one night, as his song peaked, the world lurched. Every scholar in the study house rushed to his room. His cell could not be breached. Ten men together knocked down the door. Yaakov had fallen dead in front of it, struck by the consequences of his deed. The forbidden knowledge died with him, before the pillars could topple, and the world tumble to oblivion.

The scholars, perhaps complicit for not curtailing his experiments, were quick to dispose of the evidence. Fearful of seeing the dreaded list of thirty-six, they gathered all of his papers and books in darkness. Blindly they carried his written belongings, interring them in the *genizah* beneath the synagogue, under ancient volumes turned to sod.

Rustling in their hands, the sacred list of names, some say, unsang Yaakov's sins.

This, then, was the folklore, dimly remembered, that came to mind twenty-three years ago as I worked to excavate the old German synagogue, and unearthed, beneath several feet of scriptorial sediment, a pale skin of parchment listing thirty-six people in ancient Hebrew. Already I'd observed the name Yaakov ben Eleazer on several *genizah* documents, though there must have been many Yaakovs born to Eleazers in the day, and I'd merely smiled at the coincidence that he was a scholar of Kabbalah, an amusing anecdote with which to tease my superstitious father. The skin of parchment, however, was less easily laughed away.

The thirty-six names appeared not to have been inked in lampblack, but emblazoned with fire. Moreover the lettering resembled no calligraphy I'd ever seen, let alone other writings I'd found in the Kabbalist's fervid hand. There weren't any pen strokes. Every line appeared to have been laid down at once, thirty-six names of men and women, each, in the old fashion, with a town of origin. I was well acquainted with the premodern age through my graduate research. I knew the materials and traditions. I'd seen census ledgers and divorce petitions. A list like this didn't fit.

Yet what could I say? I'd have been mad to mention Yaakov's legend to my devoutly secular colleagues, and anyway I didn't really believe, I thought, in the Lamedh-Vov. Embarrassed by my hesitation over the vellum, I slipped it under my shirt. And mortified by my impulsive theft, I kept it locked in an old suitcase for decades.

I intended to tell my father about it, to show him the list so that he could reassure me that it was not sacred, that the story of Yaakov was myth. But for five years I couldn't confess to him that I'd stolen it, and for eighteen years I couldn't admit to myself that I'd been unable to confess. Then he was dead and I was alone.

While my parents passed more than half their lives in America, my mother had insisted on burial in her family plot near Lodz. In death, my father followed her there, and I accompanied the coffin. Pressed between two starched shirts, I brought the list of thirty-six, intending finally to bury it as well. First, however, out of respect for his cherished superstitions, if not acknowledgment of my own latent beliefs, I vowed to visit one town on the list, to see if I could find any trace of saintliness.

The closest was a village of several hundred people. I set out the day after the funeral. In my rented sedan, I was conspicuous. Was I lost? Why had I come? In my adult life, I've never felt as dumb as I did then, when, as if by way of explanation, I mumbled the name of a man who'd supposedly lived there centuries before.

I was met with incredulity. Silently, I was brought to the tavern by the villagers who'd found me, and poured a draft of beer. They repeated my words to the aged barkeep. Her voice, barely audible at first, gradually recovered youth as she told me an old folktale, localest of local legends, about a fool with that name.

I missed my return flight, rescheduled twice. I lived in that village for weeks. I asked all the people who'd ever heard the legend to relate it as they remembered it. I asked each of them if they knew any of the other names on my list. I asked if they'd ever heard of Yaakov ben Eleazer. They had not. Yet when I told them the tradition of the Lamedh-Vov, they didn't find surprising the inclusion of their local idiot, whose foolishness, they believed, brought the village wisdom.

Naturally, I was familiar with the idea that the Lamedh-Vov were people who appeared insignificant. The beauty of the tradition, perhaps its lesson, was that saintliness, unlike hero-ism, is quotidian. The Lamedh-Vov were said to be chimney sweeps and water carriers, humble folks untutored in ethics. Why not also an idiot? Thoughtless deeds, even acts deemed wicked, may do right, though the merits may never be appar-ent. Talmud instructs followers to praise God for good and evil alike. I was not one to judge a Lamedh-Vov. With copious notes and a hastily arranged sabbatical, I traveled to the next village on Yaakov's numinous itinerary.

In every town the beer was differently brewed, yet the re-sponse was similar when I named a Lamedh-Vov. People didn't think of these figures as saintly: One was a thief, another a whore, and yet another, God forbid, a false Messiah. I was sometimes unable to discern the good in their deeds, yet the villagers, hearing for the first time about the list of thirty-six, always did. And, after all, the stories had sustained them. I was merely a folkloric tourist, rolling through in a rented sedan.

Twelve villages in twelve months. I intended to return from my sabbatical with material to write an academic study of folklore and history. I thought I'd examine the epistemological status of collective memory, the ontology of living myth. I would reinvigorate my career, revive my field. My pen went dry. I had no theories, only stories.

In these pages are the dozen that I've collected, as I remember them being told. They came to me gradually, one at a time, and perhaps that is how they should be read. I'm somewhere in the world searching for others now. I have resigned my academic positions. Some will accuse me of slipping into mysticism. Others will dismiss me, itinerant that I've become, as a wandering Jew. I accept these epithets, and request only to be let go. Do not seek me. I cannot say if I'll ever return. I don't pretend to know what I'm doing, but I will follow my calling.

The reader will observe that I have omitted the saints' names. Instead I identify them by the letters of the Hebrew alphabet—alef, beit, gimmel, dalet, heyh, vov—once used to count. Perhaps I'm as touched as my poor father. These saints are long gone; others survive today. However, these old names, the fleeting knowledge of them by one man, nearly brought the world to an end. As Yaakov ben Eleazer discovered, the secrecy is sacred. These are the Lamedh-Vov. Their lives are passages in the book of the unknown.

JAY KATZ, PH.D.
February 2008

ALEF THE IDIOT

Everybody knew that Alef was a fool. By trade he was a fisherman, but folks had seen a lowly carp outsmart him. Even the fish that Alef landed seldom made it past his fellow sailors, who took turns at snookering him, to decide who among them was smartest. One might lead him to believe that the rock cod in his bucket would dry to stone, and generously offer to trade it for a worm with which to try his luck again. Another might persuade him that his flounder was no odd fish, but rather the castaway face of a diver gone too long underwater, and graciously volunteer to return it to its rightful owner. To all these propositions, Alef eagerly agreed, blessed to have friends who accepted his dim wit, and looked after him.

Alef's wife, on the other hand, was less forgiving of his shortcomings. Chaya was the daughter of a rabbi celebrated as a sage in the town where she was raised, and, while she had her mother's dark hair and stormy eyes, she'd inherited her father's luminous mind.

Since no one else in the rabbi's village had been bright enough to comprehend him, least of all his wife and sons, the rabbi had taken little Chaya into his library and taught her the sacred tongue, to have someone with whom to study all that was holy. She'd mastered Hebrew with alacrity, and had learned to argue fine points of doctrine by the time she was ten. A year later, she'd trounced her father in a dispute over laws governing seminal discharge when the Sabbath sundown was occluded by a solar eclipse, from which she'd deduced that she was wiser than anyone, and, therefore, no longer had to obey her mother.

That had resulted in arguments of an altogether different order, fought in shrieks and fits and, more than once, with a hurled pot of boiling water. Scarcely his daughter's height, and half the weight of his wife, the rabbi had studiously avoided these disputes, and even Chaya's brothers, muscular thugs several years older than she, had learned to slip out the door whenever the stormy eyes of mother and child met.

Many times while his wife was away at market, the rabbi had tried to persuade Chaya to show compassion for her, or at least to respect her, as required by law. But Chaya had contested his interpretations, and even the ancient commentaries on which he based them, with such furious logic that the rabbi had been forced each time to concede defeat. Finally he'd gone to his wife, the rebbetzin, to explain how Chaya was different from other girls, and why obedience shouldn't be expected of her. His wife hadn't needed any fancy wordplay to reply. She'd simply accused the rabbi of loving his daughter in lieu of her.

This, too, he'd been unable to deny: Chaya's body was as lithe as a serpent's, and his weakness for dark hair and stormy eyes had already, of course, been established. He'd nodded and dumbly looked on while his wife had sent for the matchmaker, to get rid of the little nuisance.

In that village, the marriage broker was famous for coupling children the day they were born. Her trick was to know folks' fortunes, and to reckon love economically, according to the supply and demand of dowry. But the rabbi had forbidden her from prematurely pairing his little Chaya: He couldn't tolerate predestination from an omniscient god, let alone a know-it-all yenta. So the old woman, sturdy like a pruned tree, had come to the rebbetzin without a suitable man.

— There must be someone.

— The locals are all taken.

— Chaya is the daughter of a rabbi.

— She comes with no dowry.

— My husband is not a rich man. But our Chaya is a pretty girl, after all.

— A pretty shrew, if you'll pardon my saying so.

— Then you see why she has to go.

— I do, I do. Perhaps I *can* help you. There's a man I've heard of who lives by the sea, and for some years has sought a bride.

— Is he crippled? Is he cruel?

— Rebbetzin, folks say that he's a fool.

The rebbetzin had laughed at that. She'd squeezed the matchmaker's hand. She might even have kissed the old maid, had the rabbi not walked in, roused by the unfamiliar sound of mirth in his house. The rebbetzin had stood, then. She'd told her husband that a suitable groom had been found.

— He lives in this town?

— There isn't a man in this village who deserves her.

— Then he is a great scholar?

— What man could be as wise as Chaya?

Naturally, the rabbi hadn't had a response. And, because he was too frail to travel, the next morning he'd stood helplessly in his doorway while his wife had put their daughter in a carriage with a loaf of bread and a note bearing the name of her betrothed. He'd waved farewell, but the girl, wrapped tight in a black shawl, hadn't even looked at him. Only out on the open road had she allowed herself, inaudible amid the horses' clamor, to loosen the cloth and pour out her tears.

. . .

Alef's fellow fishermen seldom saw his wife after their wedding. Chaya refused to mingle with the common folk, lest they mock her, cultured rabbi's daughter, for being married to the village idiot. But, as much as she dreaded their jeers, what upset her more was to hear them tease her husband: Certainly Alef was a fool, as she told him whenever he was dumb enough to utter a word in her presence, yet cuts inflicted by others, which he was too dull to feel, pained her as if she were the one being gutted. Chaya might have thought that this was just one more symptom of her humiliation, were it not accompanied by another emotion—the insatiable urge to be held by him.

Alef was a large man, framed like a boat, into which slender Chaya fit as if he'd been hewn for her. Not that she believed those old romances that for every girl in the world a special boy was born: She could refute such notions historically, philosophically, and mathematically, to name but a few possibilities. Yet none of her arguments could hold up, even for a moment, to the force of a kiss. Every night came to the same conclusion. And every morning, lying in bed long after her husband had gone fishing, she'd wonder what, for all her reason, had happened.

By evening, she'd be seething, blaming Alef for taking away her sapience and saddling her with love. She never spoke to her husband in such terms, which would have been wasted on him. Instead, each night, when he returned to their home and confessed what had become of their evening meal, she'd drag him inside and squeal: *Are you a fool?* If he tried to respond, to justify his fishlessness, she'd recite her favorite proverb in the ancient tongue: *The ignorant cannot be righteous.* Since he couldn't reckon what she was saying, he'd accept all blame and listen to her sputter and curse until, exhausted by her own fuming, she'd come to be embraced by him. Then he'd take her to bed, where their differences were what brought them together again.

Chaya's behavior bewildered Alef. Why did her feelings for him turn with the hours of the day, while he adored her with the constancy of years? What could he do not to lose her each afternoon? What was wrong with him?

He pondered these questions at sea and on land. He asked the opinion of the carp he caught, but, knowing no affection outside of spawning, they didn't respond. His fellow fishermen, on the other hand, were eager to assist him, if only he'd request their advice. Every day they asked about his wife. They inquired about her scholarship. Was she still intent to unseat the village rebbe, as she'd threatened to do following a doctrinal dispute on Alef's wedding day? Did she plan to take the old maggid's place? Or did she want to put Alef on the pulpit? At the height of his confusion, the fishermen would act as if he already were the village pontiff and ask him to deliver a sermon, and, when he stuttered that he didn't know what to say, they'd applaud him for his wisdom.

Then one day a storm grounded every sailor except for Alef. (The weather didn't bother him, as he never thought to fear it; sweeping the world of hubris, the torrents always took care to let his small vessel pass.) When he harbored in the late afternoon, the docks were all but abandoned. Only Yudel, one of the shrewdest fishers, was there, repairing his mast. He called Alef over.

— What are you doing on the water in this weather?

— I'm trying to catch some fish.

— Swells like these could swallow your boat, Alef. You're a married man. What would your wife do without you?

— I'm sure she'd get along.

— She must love you, though.

— I don't know.

— What's the matter? You can't satisfy her?

— I guess not.

— For some men, it's like that. I can tell that you're miserable. I know that you've been meaning to confide in me for a while. So I'll let you in on a secret. There is a cure for your ailment. Would you do anything for Chaya, no matter what?

When Alef shyly nodded, Yudel told him where he must go and what he must do. He insisted that Alef not see his wife first, and made him swear never to tell her where he'd been: If he did, he might not see her again. Yudel accompanied Alef to the forest floor. Then he scurried to the tavern to tell the other fishermen about the fool's errand.

Alef hiked long hours through woods midnight deep and darker than the day before creation. Wolves surrounded him, spiraling like planets through the heavens. He welcomed their stoic company, for walking through forest at night is lonely. He told them of all the fish he knew, and praised his sagacious wife. But when he told them what he was about to do on her behalf, their eyes widened and, in a blink, they scattered.

Alone again, he came to a clearing. In the moon's ancient light, he saw the silhouette of a small windowless shack, seemingly built in the cast of its own shadow. He climbed onto the deck, soft as tar beneath his boots, and pounded the door three times with his fist.

The old dybbuk who answered fit Yudel's description, as much as any description could fit such a demon. His skin seemed to be molded of the same dark substance as his home. He wore no clothes, yet only his face and hands appeared naked; on the rest of his carcass, the wrinkles of black hide hung as heavy as an overcoat.

The dybbuk invited Alef inside. A faint glow illuminated the hovel, light seeping from a barrel such as those in which herring is pickled. The demon stood back while Alef approached the vat, having never known fish to be radiant.

He stared at them for a long while. They had no eyes, nor had they scales. They were slippery and pale, protoplasmic lumps no larger than Alef's hand, sunken under a thick, clear syrup.

— Where do they come from?

— They're human.

— They don't look like people.

— That's because you've seen only the parts folks show. These are people's souls.

— Those are souls?

— The most in captivity anywhere in the world. Now tell me: What can I offer for yours, Alef? What brings you here?

— Yudel the fisherman tells me that you can help me satisfy my wife.

— You're flaccid?

— People say that I'm stupid. I don't know. Every day, my Chaya asks me if I'm a fool. I just want to give her an answer.

— You think an answer would satisfy her?

— She's a great scholar. If she has to wonder, it must be the deepest mystery.

— Yes, I see. You drive a hard bargain, but I'll do it. You'll give your soul to know if you're a fool.

The dybbuk asked Alef to take off his cloak. Then he sat the fisherman on a squat wooden stool in the middle of the room. With a tin cup, he drew some syrup from the pickling barrel and washed it over his arms. He took another draft. Pinching Alef's nose, the dybbuk poured it down his throat. As Alef choked, the demon thrust a black hand down his gullet, gripping the spasm at the nub, withdrawing a pallid gland. He held it, still heaving, in front of Alef, and then dropped it in the vat.

The room glowed much brighter than before. Alef could see that the demon's living conditions were awfully poor. He'd neither hearth nor bed. That dybbuks naturally have want of neither food nor sleep only added, in Alef's estimation, to the demon's destitution. As he took his leave, he didn't wonder, as previous victims of the dybbuk invariably had, whether giving up his soul was a foolish thing to do. After all, he'd a brick oven and straw mattress, and even a wife with whom to share them. Evidently the unblessed creature needed his soul more than he did.

Chaya waited up for Alef, restless. Ever since their wedding, she hadn't passed a night alone, and, because she'd never had occasion to miss him, she didn't appreciate that the aching she felt in every organ was but a symptom of separation, an inflammation of love. Nor did it comfort her to visit the tavern at midnight, asking if anyone had seen her husband, and to be met with derision. *Probably mistook you for a bearded clam and drowned,* the sailors jeered. Then Yudel followed her home, tried to fondle her, and offered to dive for her oyster. She hurled an iron pot at him, hitting him in the groin. He staggered back to the tavern, to drink away the pain. And what did she do? She attempted to pray.

The liturgical training that Chaya had received from her father told her what words to say, with which rituals, but, as unimpeachably as she knew how to worship in theory, the truth is that she'd never before done it in practice. Prayer was for peasants, witless folk who'd good reason to be subservient. Chaya had been dependent on no one before Alef. Only the agony of his absence brought her to her knees, on the cabin's hard dirt floor. From down there, she whispered some sacred words, found they had no substance in her mouth. She uttered others, still holier. She could not feel them on her breath. She sputtered secret incantations, heavenly formulations that mortals were never meant to possess. She couldn't even hear her own voice. She started to cry. Her throat opened. Her chest filled. Her sobbing sounded like great bells pealing, ringing in a new dawn.

She did not hear her husband return. He softly shut the door. He came close, knelt in front of her. He touched a finger to her cheek, caught a falling tear.

She screamed. She staggered backward. He wondered if she didn't recognize him, if he looked different, soulless. Had he blackened like the dybbuk? Would Chaya be upset by that? Then he heard his name. She was cursing him, her persecutor, for making her adore him, only to abandon her.

He could not say that he'd been away for her sake without divulging where he'd gone, and since she did not ask the question for which he'd so dutifully sought an answer, all that he could do, as she battered him with accusations, was to look on in dumb innocence. That only made her angrier. She invoked every curse of antiquity. *The ignorant cannot be righteous,* she screeched.

Silence is the fence around wisdom, the fool at last replied. He said it almost in a whisper, but what stunned Chaya was that he'd spoken it, flawlessly, in the ancient tongue.

— Where did you learn that, Alef?

— I'm not sure.

— It's a line from Talmud.

— The words just came to me.

— You don't even know Hebrew.

— I'm not learned.

— Yet you're speaking to me in Hebrew now.

Alef recognized that she was right. He also noticed that she'd become quiet. When he embraced her, she held him even tighter than on their wedding night, peering into his eyes with even greater wonder than when they'd first come together.

The following morning, Alef found that he knew more than Talmud. Out at the seashore, sailors pestered him with trick questions of an arithmetical nature to make him blush and stammer—if you lose four of the three fish you catch, how many are left?—but he calmly responded by giving them a lesson in negative digits. Then he unmoored his boat, and, while the others puzzled over the proofs he'd written in the sand, sailed into open waters.

He dropped his line. The string went taut. He tugged to see where it had snagged—and hauled a fluke into the boat. No sooner had he cast again than he hooked another one. He pulled in five of them, then ten. His hull was just about full when he remembered that his wife didn't like fluke, which she considered common: At their wedding, Chaya had declared that she ate only salmon. So he dropped his line, and hooked her one.

It was still early when Alef sailed back into harbor. The other fishermen were where he'd left them, quibbling. Some argued that the old dybbuk was playing with them, using soulless Alef as his puppet. Others maintained that, by forsaking his soul, Alef himself became a demon. They agreed only that Chaya must not know what had happened, must not discover where they'd let Yudel send her husband, for her pot-hurling fury raged fiercer than damnation.

Then Alef was upon them. He smiled. Nervously, they grinned. He presented each with a large fish. He gave away all that he had except for the salmon, which he proudly carried home to his wife.

He handed it to her when she opened the door. The fish was as large as her torso. She did not ask if Alef was a fool. She looked at the salmon, dripping cold water down her chest, and then at her husband, blond head beatific, crowned in sweat.

— Where did you get this fish?

— I caught it. It's the kind you like, Chaya.

— I know that. But most days you can't even land an anchovy.

— In the Talmud it says . . .

— Don't quote that book to me.

— Then mathematically speaking . . .

— What the hell is happening?

— I just know where fish are in the ocean.

— Every one?

— Even the clams.

— Those aren't fish. They're forbidden.

— I can tell which oysters have pearls.

— Those can't be eaten either. But it wouldn't be criminal to give me a few jewels.

Alef pulled a couple of oysters out of his pocket and opened them with his thumbs. From each, he plucked a little oval pearl. Later, after they'd gorged on fish and on each other's flesh, Alef laid the pearls on Chaya's cheeks, where, the night before, tears had shimmered.

He slept soundly, dreaming of quantum mechanics and relativity. By the time he awoke, his wife was no longer in bed beside him. Instead there was a note, telling him that she'd gone to visit her parents.

Chaya had not been home in the year since her wedding. She hadn't even responded to her father's letters, laden with questions she'd have been humiliated to answer and money she'd have been ashamed to spend. She wrapped herself tight in her cloak as she neared the town gate, covering her face in the manner of a foreigner, lest anybody recognize her, pathetic creature, driven away by carriage, hobbling back shoeless.

She arrived at dusk. The house was quiet. The rebbetzin had gone to market, and Chaya's brothers were now married to the daughters of a wealthy merchant, who had given each a small estate. She opened the door to her father's study, and slipped inside. Without looking up from the tract he was writing, he asked her if an omniscient being could know ignorance.

She started to answer, and then stopped. She tried a different approach, which brought her to another impasse, or perhaps the same one from a different direction. At last she confessed that she wasn't certain.

He set down his pen. With both arms, he embraced her.

— For months, I've been trying to solve this problem, Chaya. In the first month, I was certain that I could do it. In the second month, I was comforted that, if I didn't, then you would. In the third month, I became troubled that you could, yet I couldn't. And in the fourth month, I became distraught that you could, but wouldn't. Ever since then, I haven't been able to write a word in these commentaries. All year, I dreamed that you would come to me like this, break the riddle, and spring me from my trap. But now that you're here, and I hear that you don't know either, I realize that the resolution doesn't matter. I remained imprisoned by it only because I wanted to see you, but couldn't. Your father is not very wise.

— And your daughter is not very good. At least I should have written.

— Your husband's a sage, Chaya. It's right that he commands all your attention.

— Now you mock me. You know that Mama married me to a fool.

— He doesn't understand the sacred texts as well as you do?

— He was illiterate until a couple of days ago. While you were busy with your learned commentaries, Mama married me to a fisherman who . . . who . . . could be outsmarted by a lowly carp, and . . .

— Illiterate until a couple of days ago? You've been teaching him, then?

She shook her head. She told him everything that had happened. She laid two pearls on the table in front of him. She was mystified. Could he explain?

The rabbi picked up the pearls, but did not scrutinize them. Instead, he peered into his daughter's eyes. He saw that they had changed. It seemed that the light had dimmed, as he'd once observed in his own bride. Then he perceived that the fire he'd previously seen from up close was now distant, insurmountably far from him, and, for the light to reach him at all, it must be orders of magnitude brighter than before. Chaya's ardor made him shiver. He looked down and told her what the evidence made obvious: Her Alef had sold his soul to a dybbuk. Since she did not respond, he told her the consequences suffered by people who bartered their souls, the agonies that he'd witnessed, tortures that might have infected everyone had he not banished those cursed folks from the community. He reminded Chaya that life was passed down the generations by the soul's nocturnal secretions, and that, because a man without a soul could not have children, his wife could legally divorce him. Chaya said that she never would. The rabbi nodded, for it was the response that he'd expected. Then she asked him where she might meet this demon.

He stopped nodding. He stared at her. Even to utter the word *dybbuk* made him shudder, yet she wished to visit this creature as if he were a country pawnbroker.

— Chaya, you can't do that.

— Alef did.

— And look what happened to him. Nobody goes to a dybbuk, except for one reason.

— That will give me an advantage in my negotiations. Trust me, Papa. My soul is not for sale.

Chaya put her hands on his. She contained their tremor. She gave him paper on which to draw a map. He made it swiftly, without lifting his pen, as if it were a sentence. The wet ink shone in the last sunlight. She kissed her father on the cheek, and hurried into the night.

The wolves already knew of Chaya, from what Alef had

told them during his recent sojourn. They escorted her, a girl of much culture and little meat, at a respectful distance, discreetly protecting her from highway robbers and other predators who might take an interest in something other than her brains. They accompanied her to the forest clearing, where the demon was outdoors, tending his night garden. They watched her approach him, regretting that it was not in their power to guard her from her own impudence.

The dybbuk cultivated mushrooms, each one as wondrously hued as an orchid. Chaya looked over his shoulder at the one he was watering, and pronounced its name. The dybbuk dropped his cup. He'd never before heard the word spoken aloud. He asked her to say it again. She uttered the name more slowly for him. He sighed. As magnificent as his fungus was, the sound was more spectacular: He knew that, to have earned such an appellation, there must be a finer specimen of the mushroom elsewhere.

He might have enlisted Chaya's expertise on care and feeding, were it not unseemly for a demon to seek a girl's advice. Instead, he invited her inside. He held the door for her. While he pulled it shut, she peered into the pickling barrel, at a thousand sunken souls.

She asked which one was Alef's. The dybbuk shrugged. He didn't keep records. *I leave the auditing to the powers above,* he said. And then he assured her that she needn't be bashful about giving up hers: The procedure left no mark on the body, and he guaranteed lifetime confidentiality. As long as she was discreet, no one would notice any change to her except, of course, that she'd be vastly richer, or prettier, than before.

— I'm not here to sell my soul.
— Nobody leaves my cottage without making a deal.
— Would you trade a soul for pearls?
— How many gems would you like, little girl?

Chaya frowned. She took the two pearlets that Alef had

given her from a pocket in the apron of her skirt. She showed them to the demon. If he would return her husband's soul, she said, he could have the gems, both of them.

He laughed at her. He laughed like a smokestack spouting soot. He told her to close her hand. When she opened it, there were twenty pearls. And as soon as she shut it again, there were none.

— What will you take for it, then? Our hovel? Alef's boat? Would you return his soul if I offered you my body for the night?

— Don't you understand, rabbi's daughter? I'm not a shipping magnate or a real estate broker, and I'm not a playboy either. I'm a demon. Everything I want comes freely to me.

— Everything except a soul.

— So I collect them, one at a time, from folks who've had them, scarcely aware, all along. I deem myself a connoisseur.

— And I consider you a glutton.

Chaya walked out on him. She trampled through his garden, squashing exotic mushrooms, and trudged into the forest.

After several hours, morning dawned. Chaya was still in deep wood, but up ahead she saw a man. His meager flesh barely stretched skintight over his bones. He sat in the dirt, neither home nor wife in sight, surrounded by sacks such as those she'd seen ragpickers carry. She asked if he was a beggar.

— You can't help me.

Who says I'm offering? I have troubles of my own. What's in the sacks?

— The weight of my misfortune.

Chaya was a strong girl, given her slight build. She tried to lift a bag. She strained. She swore. She couldn't budge it. So she looked inside, and was blinded.

While sight seeped back into Chaya's eyes, she reached into the sack and scooped out a palmful of coins. They were unlike any she'd ever seen, even the ancient and arcane denominations in the synagogue coffers. She could not decipher the inscriptions on them, nor could she identify the species of beast adorning the face of each. Curiouser, though, was the substance, as soft and sticky as honey.

As the bullion warmed in her palm and trickled through her fingers, she marveled at the purity of the metal.

— It's twenty-five-karat gold. That's what I get for selling my soul.

— Then you, too, visited the dybbuk last night?

— Last night? I was there a decade ago. It's taken ten years just to haul my hoard this far into the forest.

— Why don't you leave it, if it's only a hindrance?

— Without my soul, this burden is all I've got. The burden of my greed. And what did you take in exchange for your soul?

— I didn't sell.

— Then you're a very fortunate girl. All through these woods, you'll come across folks who bartered theirs.

— Are they hard to find? Do you know them well?

— What do I have to share with other people? We keep to ourselves.

Chaya soon found that the man had spoken truly. She saw many folks, always alone, some up in trees, others huddled on the ground. They shied like untame animals as she passed. She paused to gaze at a woman crouched in a bush. The girl wore nothing but dust and shadows. Blackberry brambles grew in her hair. Yet, even at a distance, Chaya could see that the girl's softness would be the envy of a princess, and that her ripe lips could seduce a king. Chaya remarked that the girl was more beautiful than any she'd ever met, and felt tingling inadequacy in her own flesh. Glancing back at Chaya, the girl began to weep.

— What's the matter?

— You can't help me.

— I met a man who sold his soul for gold too heavy to carry. But what could be the burden of beauty?

— You've no idea. Before I went to that cursed dybbuk, I was an old hag. I lived by a lake, and I'd spit at my ugliness every day when I knelt to drink. Sometimes at dusk, peasant girls would come to bathe. They'd splash and play, and I'd imagine what a happy life I'd lead if I were pretty. That demon didn't just snatch my soul, you see. When he gave me this flesh, he took away my dreams.

— But you could go to town and marry any man you wished.

— Marry? I'm a hundred years old, girlie.

Slowly she stood. Her back was bent, her legs bowed. She clamped a hand on Chaya's arm, brittle bones quivering in their new skin.

— Do you still think I'm such a beauty? When the dybbuk took my soul, he left an emptiness. The ugliness festers there, where I can't even spit on it.

Chaya shuddered. She pulled away and hurried home, horrified by the miseries that Alef must be suffering as his soullessness sank in. She steadied herself as she neared their hovel. Whatever his condition, she vowed not to put him down: Irredeemably foolish as he'd been in his diabolical dealings, she would not call him a fool again. She opened the door. And found him humming to himself, cooking up a bouillabaisse.

Was Alef so stupid as not to be afflicted? Was he so smart? Chaya was befuddled, and more so by the bouillabaisse, which wasn't even native to their region. She asked if he knew what he was doing. He shrugged and made her sushi.

He did not inquire where she'd been all night long. After supper, he simply brought her to bed and showed her how much he'd missed her. What could be said? In the essential respects, she had to confess, Alef was the same.

Only the implications were different. Instead of giving up one fish, or even a dozen, Alef handed out a hundred. He was equally free with his advice. He showed carpenters how to frame their houses taller, farmers how to plow their fields deeper, and millers how to motorize their operations, a plan that had to be scuttled for want of electricity. Day after day, Chaya watched her husband cure diseases and adjudicate disputes.

It was harder for her than when he'd been the town laughingstock. Everything he knew taught her all that she did not. And what was the benefit? In the corner of the hovel, stewing like a bouillabaisse, she'd watch him dole out fish by the bucket while giving away ideas that made other folks' fortunes: An anesthetic. Movable type. An assembly line. By evening her vow would be broken in all but name, as she berated Alef for stupidly helping strangers fleece him while he neglected his own devoted wife. To these complaints he'd respond not with words but with pearls, which he'd string together with kisses until all was well.

At last a rich merchant from the city, who'd heard rumors of Alef's genius, paid him a visit, and begged his expertise: The merchant wanted to know how to transmute lead into gold. As the fisherman began to answer, Chaya sprang from her chair, and, screaming obscenities that would turn platinum into iron, chased the knave out the door. She stared at her husband, eyes ablaze. *You are a fool,* she hissed.

Alef nodded. A smile enveloped his face.

— For a long time, I didn't know, Chaya. You asked me every day, and I couldn't tell you until finally I went to the dybbuk to find out.

— You didn't have to do that.

— I did, though. It's no simple question, like how to create gold. To comprehend what I don't understand depends on knowing all there is to know.

— Alef, that's nonsense.

— To discover the leak in a bucket, you have to fill it, Chaya. At first I thought that the dybbuk had misunderstood my wish, but the more wisdom I dispense, the more I find what my head never held.

— And you aren't tormented by that?

— A fool is never tormented. Torment isn't about what you don't know. It's about what you have and can't give.

After that, Chaya no longer interfered with Alef's generosity. Instead, she tried to emulate it. She found that giving was an effort, that, even with her impressive intellect, she couldn't do as well as Alef did in his simplicity. She envied his foolishness. All night long she clung to him as her sole source of meaning.

And in the morning she'd go out into the forest to tend to the soulless. She'd bring them fish, which she taught them how to cook into a bouillabaisse. She'd tell them that they didn't have to be tortured. She'd patiently explain that the torment they felt, they inflicted on themselves. They consumed her fish, but rejected her logic. They said that to believe the soul was insignificant, she must surely have lost her sense.

One day, after Chaya had given away every fish in her basket, she found herself near where the dybbuk lived. She decided to visit.

She stepped onto his deck, which seeped through her toes in the afternoon heat. She called out the demon's name. He opened his door a crack, squinting into the sun, trying to ascertain whether the heavens were in flames. Then he saw, standing on his stoop, hands on hips as if she were a neighbor, little Chaya.

— Don't you see that it's the middle of the day? I'm a creature of the night. What do you have in the basket?

— It's empty. There were fish in it.

— I've never tasted fish. You can't imagine what it's like having a mouth but no appetite.

Chaya looked at the demon under the bright sun. His black hide shimmered with sweat, but his mouth was a void that trapped even light. His was a deeper hunger.

— Do you still want my soul? I've decided that you can have it.

— What will you take in exchange? You're pretty, but I can make you a queen.

— No, thank you.

— You're clever, but I can make you a goddess.

— I'll give you my soul, but I don't want anything for it.

— Perhaps you're not so shrewd after all.

In a single stroke, he reached his hand down Chaya's throat and pulled her slender soul out. He brought it inside and plunged it, still breathing, into his vat. Then, because he wished her to have something in return, he showed her the exotic spiders he kept, ruby and emerald cabochon gems skittering around on their eight-point crowns. He offered her any one she liked. They climbed across his knuckles. He fancied that he'd never looked so princely. He didn't even see Chaya wave good-bye.

Years passed. As Alef and Chaya aged together, each grew to fill the space in the other where there'd been a soul before. They never discussed it, for they'd become too intimate for words. And nobody else noticed, so busy were they taking all that the couple gave.

Folks prospered. Their village became a town. Fine houses were built, and neighbors complained about Alef's ungainly hovel. The fool and his wife moved into the slums. What fish they didn't give away was stolen. But that just saved them the hassle of distribution.

One evening they were visited by a very old man. While people often still came to profit from Alef's knowledge, none looked as needy as this fellow. He wore a heavy old cloak and hat, and walked with a crook as knotted as his crippled body.

Chaya brought him a chair. She couldn't see his face under the hat's broad brim, but, the instant his eyes met hers, she felt sure that she'd encountered him before. She asked the man if there was something they could do for him.

He shook his head. It was winter and getting dark, and he simply wished for a place to rest.

Chaya went to Alef, who was standing by the hearth, ladling bouillabaisse into a copper cup. She brought it to their guest. She sat by him while Alef prepared the bed in the adjoining room, where he and Chaya slept, so that the man could pass the night in comfort. The visitor didn't talk. He raised the cup to his mouth several times, but, when he set it down, it was always still full. Chaya asked if there was another meal that he'd prefer, anything at all. Or perhaps there was some ailment he had, and Alef could tell him the cure for it. He shook his head again. She thought she heard him sigh, though it might have been the winter wind sweeping by.

Alef helped him to bed, and bade him a good night. The guest lay down on the straw mattress without removing cloak or hat. He pretended to sleep. And then he really did.

Some hours later, he was awoken by a noise in the other room. Without moving, he strained to hear if the couple was speaking of him. But the utterances weren't in any ordinary language. He concentrated on each syllable until it came to him that the two of them weren't making conversation. They were making love.

He waited awhile, until they were quiet. He waited some time more. He gripped his crook. Slowly he stood up. He stepped out of the bedroom.

The couple lay on the floor by the hearth, entwined in

sleep. In the embers' glow, he could see that they were naked. Alef's hands, creased with years, folded over Chaya's shoulders. Her gray hair fell across his chest like an early frost. Their ancient guest crouched close. He saw the faint line of a smile where their wrinkled faces touched.

He went away before the light arrived. At the foot of the forest, he dropped his crook. Coming into the clearing where he lived, he tossed away his hat and cloak. The dybbuk went home more mystified than he'd been when he'd left.

He peered inside his pickling barrel. Ever since Chaya had freely given up her soul, he'd wondered whether having such a thing was really so valuable. He'd comforted himself with the torments of the soulless folks who wandered in the forest. But to look at Chaya and Alef... He gazed into his vat, and he no longer saw what he'd wanted.

The demon neglected his great occupation after that. He concerned himself with his collection of precious spiders, and with cultivating mushrooms in hues that illuminated the night. These hobbies pleased him. He grew so affable that the wolves no longer feared him. They visited often, serenading the brightest orbs in his night garden as if he were raising new moons.

Gradually the pickling barrel dried out. The wood warped and cracked. The glands shriveled. The dybbuk didn't even notice as they dissipated, and the forest dwellers dwindled.

At last, only the souls of Alef and Chaya remained. They shrunk into each other, creasing into a faint smile. And as they lost substance, some say, the demon's own soullessness passed away.

BEIT THE LIAR

One day, a peasant named Beit foretold a cataclysmic flood. She'd been lying in a field, tending the local noble's sheep, when sleep overcame her, and she felt her body float away, as if on water.

To most folks, the meaning of Beit's dream was clear: Peasant families in the valley promptly hauled everything they could up the nearest hillside. But the local noble, whose celestial observations forecast conditions as dry as the charts on which his learned astrology relied, forbade his servants from so much as thinking about the weather.

When the rains came, he'd no time to reconsider. While well fortified against human intruders, his castle couldn't hold back the water, nor could he take command of the rising river, for it was a tributary of the king. All his property was washed away—sheep and servants and star charts—and he saved his family only by barricading them in the celestial observatory, where raindrops the size of gunshot pelted them while they gazed down upon their ruptured legacy.

Several days passed before the land dried, the river returned to its bed, and the peasants came home again. By then the noble had chosen an appropriate retribution for their desertion: Beit's prediction had brought on his misfortune, so he'd have the girl hanged in front of them. He demanded that they surrender her. But they couldn't comply, as she'd already been seized by the king.

Nobody could say how word of Beit's witchcraft had so swiftly reached His Majesty. No one knew by which route she'd been taken away. The noble had no official recourse. An avowed pragmatist, he had to satisfy himself with the thought that, even if he couldn't get his own rope around her throat, the king's hangman was an old hand at noosing insolent little peasant girls.

Yet justice is never so simple: Far from dead in the royal gallows, Beit slept that night in the king's palace, high on a feather bed, in a cloud of down pillows.

Her first audience with His Majesty had taken place in his stables, amid the dust of her arrival from the countryside. He was a young king, and brash. (He'd banned music because the notes couldn't be played all at once, and also dance, which he deemed needlessly circuitous.) In the midnight dark, he'd scarcely noticed Beit's filthy freckled peasant face or her tattered burlap frock. He'd fixed his gaze on her turquoise eyes and demanded that she explain her gypsy tricks.

— I was tending sheep. I fell asleep.
— Then you're a seer.
— I like to dream.
— From now on, your dreams are mine.

She'd merely shrugged in reply, and, by the time she thought to ask the king a few questions of her own, His Majesty was gone.

· · ·

In the morning, two maids bathed her, and, while they combed her hair, a seamstress fitted her in a white silk gown. The fabric was lighter, and cooler, than her own bare skin, and, after the servants left her, she had to keep glancing in the mirror to make sure she was not standing stark naked, as she'd heard happened to certain emperors.

Her reflection delighted her. She'd never encountered a looking glass before, and had so little sense of her own appearance that it counted as a new friend. How much more entertaining it was than Beit's peasant family: She and her reflection spun themselves dizzy, and exchanged more curtsies than she could count. Then luncheon was served, a feast for one, set on a cloth of fine linen, and it was late afternoon by the time she thought to leave her room. She slid on a pair of kidskin slippers. She set out to explore her realm.

Beit had no recollection of the palace from the night before, its marbleized vastness and gilded splendor, and still less did she recognize, in crown of state and clutch of courtiers, the prickly little king she'd met in the stables. He beckoned her. He presented the peasant girl to his retinue. He bade her tell him the future.

— The future?

— I want to know your dreams.

— I slept so well, Your Majesty. I think I didn't have any.

— Will you tonight?

— How would I know?

— You disappoint me, Beit. See that it doesn't happen again.

A sentry returned her to her room and locked the door behind her. She looked at her reflection in the mirror. No longer was it so much fun. She might even have missed her family, were it not for her new silk gown and the royal accommodations. Then came supper, a beef roast served with a carafe of wine, from which she drank until she felt giddy again: Most girls dreamed of being princesses, and here she practically was one.

That night Beit took care not to sleep so soundly, to be sure she'd have visions for the king. She set aside all her quilts and pillows. Yet, even sprawled across bare mattress board, Beit passed the night in one blind stretch.

While the maids made no comments about her odd nocturnal habits when they brought her breakfast, they couldn't help but gasp the following morning, upon finding her asleep on the stone-cold floor. As they brushed Beit's hair, the younger, who went by the name Leah, asked if she didn't care for the amenities in His Majesty's palace. Beit shook her head and then, before Leah could catch it, a tear dropped into the girl's silken lap.

— I don't dream anymore.

— Living like this, who'd need to, miss?

— Me, if I don't want to upset His Majesty.

— In that case, why not pretend?

— He'd know, because it wouldn't come true.

— Tell him he'll eat pheasant for supper tonight.

— How do you know?

— My fiancé works in His Majesty's pantry. He always tells me what scraps we'll soon be eating.

While Leah tied up Beit's braids, the other maid, who was called Ruth, counseled the girl to be careful: Beit might be expelled if she admitted that her visions had left her, but Ruth had spent enough years in the king's employ to witness the execution of a dozen seers who'd misperceived the future.

His Majesty came to Beit's room that afternoon. The sentry opened her door. She was sitting on the floor, absently toying with a bit of satin ribbon the maids had left there. She

looked up. Behind the king stood a full complement of courtiers, arranged, in colored livery, by degree of royal favor.

The king snatched the ribbon from Beit's fingers. He tied it
in a noose.

— Is this a new method of divination? Peasants are the
strangest creatures. Come, my little girl. Won't you tell us the
future?

Beit glanced at the noose in his hands. She touched her
throat. And then she looked around the room, at the canopy
bed as capacious as the hovel in which her whole family lived,
and the marble table where were served, for her delectation
alone, meals hearty enough to feed her entire town. She took in
the mirror, its reflection of her dimpled round face, crowned in
braids fancier than those worn by the local noble's daughters,
her plump body frocked in silk finer than the fabric in which
the noble cloaked his wife. She met the king's gaze with her
turquoise eyes.

— I dreamed of pheasants.

— What about them?

— There were many, maybe a hundred. They all landed,
one at a time, in small round ponds, and nothing under the sun
could make them rise again.

— But, you fool, pheasants live on land.

— I'm sure Your Majesty is right. I'm just a senseless peasant. Who can say what my visions mean?

The king didn't answer. He just laughed at her. He slipped
the noose onto his pinky, and pulled on it until the ribbon
snapped. After that, he left Beit.

Just before the sentry shut the door, the last in His Majesty's
retinue picked up the bits of satin from the floor. Putting them
in her hands, he whispered that he, at least, felt for her.

You believe in my dreams?

— Those don't matter.

— They're all I have.

— Not necessarily.

— Without dreams, I'm just a peasant. You were born a noble. You can't understand.

— My mother was a court seer. After her visions faltered, my father was noble enough to save me, but not her.

— What do you feel for me, then?

— I don't feel alone.

The king was still carrying on about the dumb shepherd girl, and how ignorant she was of birds, when supper was served. He sat at the head of a table so long that guests arrived on horseback, and messengers carried conversation, inscribed on slates of ivory, from chair to chair. He sank fork and knife into his meat. He took a bite.

— What is this food?

— Pheasant, Your Majesty.

The king raised his eyes from his plate. He watched servants set down dishes in front of his ninety-nine guests. He dropped his silverware.

— Small round ponds.

— What did His Majesty say?

— They all landed, one at a time, in small round ponds, and nothing under the sun could make them rise again.

— Is His Majesty reciting poetry?

The king stood. He ordered that Beit be sent to the dungeon, and served only gruel. Then he shut himself in his rooms.

In her cold stone cell, Beit no longer had to worry about sleeping too deeply for dreams to reach her. She couldn't even find a place to rest her head. She paced to keep away the rats, and periodically warmed her cheeks with tears.

At around midnight, she heard footsteps on the staircase, met by the gendarme assigned to guard her. The visitor spoke to her jailer in a familiar voice, lower than the king's, and softer. The soldier let the man pass, and Beit saw, approaching her rusty cage, one of His Majesty's entourage: the courtier who'd felt for her. She'd scarcely noticed his visage when they'd last met, the sad dark face behind great fronds of mustache. Now he was all she had, a liveried aristocrat outside her cell, pressing against the grille, as if he were *her* prisoner.

— You must be hungry. I've brought food from His Majesty's table.

— What is it?

— Pheasant.

— Then I was right. You've come to free me?

— I would if I had a key. You made a fool of the king, Beit. Be grateful you're not dead.

— He wanted to know the future.

— He never knows what he wants until he's had it already. But I've spent nights down here. Everyone does, now and then. Eventually he'll come around.

— When?

— He leaves tomorrow for a week. His moods improve with travel.

— I can't survive here that long.

— You're a peasant.

— I was one. Where's he going? Can't it wait?

— He's riding to the mountains, to build a castle.

— What's wrong with this one? Aside from the dungeon.

— Who knows, Beit? I have to go. If His Majesty finds me with you, he'll hang us both on the same rope.

— Please just tell me your name?

— You can call me Chaim.

Then he was gone. She shared her pheasant with the rats, on the condition that they stop harassing her, but, when the food was done, they pretended to have made no such bargain. She couldn't lie down or even sit. Lazy Beit had never stood so long in her life as she did that night.

The king came to her at dawn, before embarking on his trip. He was alone.

— You tried to humiliate me, Beit. You know that's a crime.

— Your Majesty asked for a prediction. Perhaps you'd like another one?

— I would not.

— Last night I dreamed of a man who tried to lay the sky with stone.

— And . . . what happened?

— It tumbled down on him.

— Could it have been a castle? Up on a mountain?

— I don't know, Your Majesty. I didn't have a good view. It isn't easy sleeping underground.

Beit was given a suite of three rooms with a balcony overlooking the royal gardens, and, in place of a sentry, a pair of footmen. They brought her cheese and grapes, which she ate while Ruth and Leah tended to her braids, and Elke the seamstress took her orders for a whole silken wardrobe.

Chaim found her there. (Every marble vault in the royal court reverberated with rumors of her restored fortunes, the king's abandoned building plans.) She received the courtier with a lady's grace, and offered him a bunch of purple grapes. She told him about the glorious gowns she'd have soon. Then she asked him, coy like a courtesan, where the king planned now to erect his new castle. Chaim had no answer. She took back her fruit, and suggested he find out. She turned to Elke. She asked when she could expect her couture. The seamstress told her that His Majesty immediately required a new doublet suitable for a fox hunt, but promised her a gown that would garner marriage vows in time for the upcoming pageant.

Beit supped at the royal table that night, where the king toasted her talent as a seer, and asked what new visions she had to share. She frowned. She took a gulp of port. Then, fixing his gaze with her turquoise eyes, she told him of a fox who so admired the cut of a hunter's silk jacket that it gave up its own fur coat.

Before the courtiers could laugh at her, the king asked if the hunter was wearing a red doublet. She nodded sagely. Triumphant, he commanded his retinue never again to doubt Beit. He ordered them to venerate her.

They obeyed. She'd no need of new gowns, so tightly did they cling to her. The gossipy patter of their flirtation gave her fodder for a thousand and one dreams with which to amuse His petulant Highness. For a man who has no time for history, an oracle is the ultimate entertainment, and it made no difference to the king whether Beit foretold the apocalypse or the names of that evening's supper guests, as long as the prediction proved correct.

Everyone adored Beit. Only Chaim was distraught by her behavior, the way she wallowed in courtly rumor, teasing it from men beneath an abundance of cleavage, letting them caress her wherever they pleased, as long as they whispered fresh intrigues in her ear. He was as impressed as anyone by her foresight, naturally, yet he wondered when, given all the revelry that consumed her night and day, she even had time to dream.

Chaim had time aplenty, and, in his sleep, Beit was always with him alone, far from the courtiers he'd grown up with, or the palace where he'd been born. She was a shepherdess again, he a woodsman, and their whole wealth was in children, a veritable kingdom of them. The only trouble was that, unlike Beit's charmed dreams, poor Chaim's never came to pass.

In fact, since Chaim had no talent for gossip, Beit barely noticed him anymore. His lowly social rank ensured that he was never seated near her at supper. Occasionally, he found her with other courtiers in the gardens—stumbled over a foursome of feet entangled in the hedgerow—but such circumstances proved unsuitable for conversation. If he wanted her attention again, much less to share his dreams with her, he'd need a miracle, or at least a good scandal.

He attended more closely to the king. He lingered while His Majesty received ministers and soldiers and foreign emissaries. And not more than a week passed before he had his wish.

He wished immediately that he hadn't. For his miracle, the scandal, concerned Beit's native land, where—whether by chance or design—the king had found a mountain suitable for his castle in the sky. Chaim watched as His Majesty summoned the local noble, and offered, by way of compensation for the land, the peasants of the region as serfs, to be property of his family in perpetuity. Ever since the flood, the noble had needed free labor more than pretty scenery. He agreed.

Late that night, Chaim found Beit in her rooms, asleep atop a bed so high he had to climb a ladder. He drew back the lace canopy and gazed at her, softer and stiller than the litter of pillows surrounding her. He grasped her hand, sending a wisp of expectation across her lips. She opened her eyes. Wide.

— Who invited *you* up here?
— I have to talk to you.
— Now?
— It's about the king.
— I already know everything.
— You know he's selling your family into slavery?
— I don't have family here, silly. I'm practically royalty. Is this your idea of gossip?

— Everyone in your village has been given to the local noble, in exchange for a mountain where His Majesty is going to build his alpine castle.

— You're boring me, Chaim. Please go away.

Beit turned her head and shut her eyes. But the sleep that embraced her wasn't gentle anymore. She was assaulted by nightmares. Folks she'd known before filed by in tattered work-clothes. She called to them, but they didn't answer. She saw that they'd neither eyes nor ears. Then she heard what she was saying: *Are you my family?*

When Leah woke her, Beit was sure that what Chaim had told her was true. She needed to see him immediately, not so much to ask him questions as to say that she felt what he did. But she couldn't slip away. The maids had her by the braids and the seamstress was lacing her in a gown, for the day of the pageant had come.

Revelers arrived from every town and village in the kingdom. Nobles and merchants and peasants shared the streets, and even exchanged greetings, all distinctions flattened in the shadow of His Majesty's palace.

The pageant was the monarch's annual tribute to his own benevolence, funded by a nonproductivity tax he assessed against sleep. All day long, his subjects tirelessly ate mutton cooked on iron spits and drank wine by the bucket, while he addressed them from a pedestal up on his castle's grand balcony.

That year, after observing them awhile from the overhead perspective he found so agreeable, he decided to give them an unexpected treat. He had Beit brought to the balcony to relate, in front of everybody, her latest dream. Beit was legendary by then, the country's first celebrity, and, while the king had to shout to get attention, her small voice silenced the whole city. She blinked her turquoise eyes. And found, effortlessly, Chaim's gaze.

— Are you sure Your Majesty wants to know what I've foreseen?

— Of course I do. Why else would I call for you?

— I dreamed . . .

— Dreamed what?

— Dreamed that Your Majesty secretly sold my whole village into slavery just to build another showy castle.

— You don't know what you're talking about. You never have visions like that.

— In my dream, you stole my family's freedom, made them serfs of the local noble, and I have a premonition, Your Majesty, that you'll do it to other people as well.

— It's a lie, Beit. Your dreams deceive you.

— Everybody knows they always come true.

— You're a fool. Would you stake your life on this?

— Yes.

The king's subjects no longer stood by idly, gnawing on His Majesty's spit-fired offal. Peasants were shouting, as nobles shuffled behind castle walls for royal protection until the masses were oppressed again. The king could barely be heard over the din. He cursed Beit. He begged his subjects to trust him. He bade them see for themselves that she was wrong, demanded that the peasants send a delegation to her town. He offered them horses, the swifter to be done with this business, and sent Beit to the dungeon again, lest she try to run from the inevitable.

Nobody visited her prison. Armed sentries blocked the stairs. When the rats came, she'd no food to share. She gave them her lace collar, with which they made a nest where they could leer at her in leisure. In timeless darkness, where hours loitered for weeks, she didn't know how many days passed without sleep, and couldn't recollect when she was overcome with delirium. She stared at her hands, the translucent blue skin—and then she saw nothing at all.

A bag over her head . . . Men's voices . . . Special commission . . . Thorough investigation . . . No truth to Beit's prediction . . . Formal charges: treason . . . To the gallows . . . Beit the liar . . . ! Death to her . . . ! Death to her . . . !

They marched Beit several miles, every step a stumble. They prodded her with sticks while she walked, and pelted her with rocks when she fell. They bloodied her like a martyr. And cursed her like the devil.

The gallows stood on a bridge, river underfoot, and rope overhead. The hangman noosed her neck, under her burlap hood. The king stepped forward, and asked if, in her present condition, there was anything else she'd care to predict. She heard herself answer with what sounded like pique, but she knew was not, for it had come in her delirium: the sensation of floating again. She told His Majesty that the rope would snap.

— Snap your little neck, my pretty.

— I've lied before. But my future is no longer yours.

The king stepped in front of the hangman. He threw the lever that dropped the trap under her feet. She fell. The rope went taut. And slack.

The king's sentries would not follow her into the river, a dizzying drop into rapids that frothed as if rabid, and were known to swallow men whole. The king's archers lowered their arrows. Nor would His Majesty issue orders to pursue her. For hours, some said days, he stared at the broken rope, mute.

Of course, others talked. By the time Beit's battered body reached her native village, and her brothers dragged her from the water, the whole country knew of her latest feat. They no longer called her a liar, but questioned the honesty of their monarch.

The local noble wouldn't come near her, yet hundreds of others visited while she convalesced. She slept for a year, and then two more. Folks speculated on her dreams, then lost interest, as ever more of the future slipped past. Finally only one man remained, a stranger who some claimed (based on his fronds of mustache and awkward speech) had been born a courtier. He fed her broth and hummed lullabies in her ear.

Then, one day, when he was alone with her, she opened her turquoise eyes, and grasped his hand.

— Chaim?

— Yes?

— Am I asleep?

— Not anymore.

— Are you also awake?

— As never before.

As the years passed, the couple came to feel as one. Finally all that separated them were Beit's dreams, a lapse that grew unbearable in their otherwise seamless existence. One night, she whispered to him about the years she'd slept, and why they'd gone on so long: She'd been a shepherdess again, he a woodsman, and their whole wealth was in children.

All of that happened, he reminded her, exactly as she'd described. She quieted him. She said that the dream, her vision, ended like this. She held his hands. And, together, they felt their lives float past.

GIMMEL THE GAMBLER

Into a kingdom as small and orderly as a widow's vegetable garden once wandered a peddler named Gimmel. He was not an ordinary tradesman, for he carried no goods with him. He'd neither the customary donkey nor cart, and folks scarcely noticed him at first. But in a country as orderly as this (even tombstones were alphabetical), and as tidy (even the forest floor was swept), a man without evident purpose was bound to make people curious.

On market day, they found Gimmel apart from the other peddlers, sitting on the ground with a couple of coins in hand. *Are you a lender?* they asked. *A money changer?* (While they had no need for either, never living beyond their means, nor traveling far, they'd occasionally heard tradesmen mention such exotic professions.) He shook his head. He was a gambler, he said. A peddler of chance.

They considered him more closely, then. Traders were a rough breed, naturally, but Gimmel made the others look like burghers: He lacked an eye, and three fingers on one hand. He'd no hair on his head, and his skin was burnished like a workman's apron where it wasn't covered up with an old burlap sack. And yet he was so perfectly oblivious to the misfortunes that had befallen his flesh, it made scant impression on those he met. None of the people gathered around him asked why his ear was torn, how his nose got bent. *What's a gambler?* they wanted to know. *What's a chance?*

From his tobacco pouch, Gimmel took two small gems. He showed people how both were cut the same, perfect cubes of clear green, each facet drilled with a different pattern. Sides numbered one to six, he explained, letting folks examine. All approved of their evident orderliness. He cupped the stones again and said they were dice.

— You sell them?

— You roll them.

— Why?

— So that you've something to bet on.

Gimmel found that it wasn't easy to explain betting to these people, who had never known anything but certainty. First he compared it to choosing which crop to plant without being sure when summer would come, but in their country they had calculations that named the seasons in advance, to eliminate risk. Then he took love as an analogy: You gamble on the girl you wed. That confused them still more, for all marriages were equally desireless, to eradicate covetousness.

The country was too rigidly defined for metaphor. So Gimmel decided to demonstrate instead. He showed how to lay money down, guess what number will come up, and toss.

— How can you be certain of which way they'll fall?

— You can't, unless you're a cheat.

— What's a cheat?

— Someone who'd rather win than bet.

Gradually he taught a few people the game. When folks wanted to bet on the number one, because it came first, he had to show them that two dice always add up to double that. Thus he earned their respect: Never before had they encountered a tradesman who was also a mathematician.

Money passed back and forth all afternoon in his corner of the market square, without a thought of cows or bushels of wheat: Gambling was not only entertaining but also worry-free, and soon Gimmel was more mobbed than all the other peddlers combined. Chance, pure as gold and free as air, was the kingdom's latest luxury.

Gimmel came out just enough ahead that evening to buy some supper, with a coin left over to gamble the following morning. He strolled into the forest, where the floor was as smooth and soft as a rich man's bed. He lay on his back, and fell asleep counting constellations, God's dice roll with the universe.

In this country, the king was a very busy man. All day and night he dragged a wooden ladder back and forth across the floor of his palace library, researching. Years before, he'd tried assigning some of the work to advisers, but none of them could be relied on to assign every word its right weight, let alone to extract from whole passages their exact measure. In those books were encoded the rules by which the country ran, traditions so precisely honed that the whole kingdom could be torn asunder by a single error, as an entire mill can break down on account of one faulty pin. Every conceivable subject was contained in those books, a thousand volumes, each as heavy as a man could lift.

They walled the room, a fortress of tradition, which, aside from the ladder, had as furniture only a table large enough to support one tome.

Most of the king's day was spent looking up routine matters, such as whether the forest floor had to be scrubbed with soap after a rainstorm. Grateful as the king was for not needing to make such decisions, other cases were horribly complicated by the number of precedents that simultaneously had to be taken into consideration.

One in particular bedeviled him, and had rattled his nocturnal hours, as persistent as a succubus, for many years: the selection of his own bride. Not a single matter was more important to his subjects, for whom there could be no future until he had an heir. Muscular as his arms were from lifting books, and lithe as his fingers were from flipping pages, he was no longer young. He wore the same cerulean robes that he had for as long as folks could remember, but the seasons had crowned him, in his fortieth year, with a silver head of hair.

His Majesty looked like a sage, a philosopher-king of antiquity, but truly the effect didn't reach beneath his coif. While he knew he had to marry the most worthy girl in the land, he'd no idea how to calculate who best fit that description. There were so many variables to factor into the equation: lineage, social status, wealth, intelligence, beauty. And to look up in his books any one condition was to discover variables within variables, a tyranny of details. How to evaluate lineage when family trees were brambles of intermarriage? How to assay wealth when gold held weight only in proportion to the whole economy?

With each passing year, the king was less confident than he'd been the year before. If anything, that made him a better administrator. He had no prejudices. He made no assumptions. He spoke without inflection. When told of Gimmel, whose second day in the marketplace drew an even rowdier crowd than the first, he showed no personal aversion. With customary resignation, he said that he'd have to consult his books.

In his thousand hide-bound volumes, the word *gambler* wasn't mentioned once. He couldn't even find a definition for *chance*. Finally, he asked that Gimmel be brought to his library.

— Your Majesty wants to play?

— Tell me, what is it you do for a living?

The king watched as the gambler rolled two dice across his little table, and then rolled them again. Each time, a different number came up. The king stared, incredulous.

— Is it a trick?

— If it were, Your Majesty, they'd always show up the same.

He invited the king to place a bet. Each would pick a number, and the one whose guess came closer would win the pot. Of course, the monarch had never made a guess in his life, but, after consultation with a couple of books, he reckoned that the highest number was the only one worthy of a sovereign. He bet that the dice would roll twelve. Gimmel, on the other hand, picked the number that brought him the best luck: He put his money, the last penny he had, on seven. The king tossed. The gambler won.

Was His Majesty upset? Not in the least. In fact, he felt the faint lightness in his head, the slight tingling in his fingers, that occasionally came to him when he stood at the top rung of his ladder, reaching for a book almost out of reach. He ordered another round.

They played for hours. Gradually, the library filled with the king's treasure, which he steadily lost to Gimmel. The gambler was especially fortunate that day, right on the money. Just to be fair, he suggested that the king bet on lucky seven, but his majesty preferred consistency. And perhaps he enjoyed losing his fortune, unspent by tradition, centuries' burden.

By the next morning, the king's coffers were empty. He'd gambled away all the crown jewels, every grain of silver and gold. He wanted to wager his books, but he knew they no longer had value. So he grasped Gimmel's hands.

— Enjoy my fortune. For what you've given me, it's scarcely compensation.

Two wagons were brought to haul the treasure away. The king had them hitched with horses from the royal stables. He also offered a rank of guards, but the gambler preferred to take his chances. The monarch nodded, understanding. He held out the horses' reins to Gimmel. Before the gambler took them, he reached into his tobacco sack. He took out the dice, and handed them to the king.

His Majesty gazed at the dice, radiant in sunlight. He vowed that the girl he married should have eyes so green. When he looked up again, Gimmel was gone.

The first frost of winter came fast and hard that year, a month ahead of schedule according to the palace calendar. Folks came to their king in confusion. Nothing like this had happened for as long as anyone could remember. Whole crops faced failure. *What should we do?* the peasants begged to know.

After viewing the countryside, His Majesty retreated to his library. He could count at least a dozen volumes that addressed such problems, advising prudence: Crops should be harvested at once, lest all be lost, and supplemented by foreign grain, purchased by the crown. The king looked up at his shelves, then down at his dice on the table. He grasped the gems and threw them, a gamble on the coming weather. They came up lucky seven. He told his subjects not to harvest yet.

That night, clouds clustered, heavy with snow. Farmers boarded up their barns. But the blizzard didn't come. Morning brought warm sun. Crops got another week of autumn, then two more. Nobody starved that year.

Meanwhile, the king found other uses for his dice. In fact, he never consulted his books anymore. He left every decision to chance. Must houses all be white? Must all roads be straight? Must every tree be trimmed to the same height? Not anymore, they didn't. And if everything could be any which way, why even roll dice in the first place?

No longer was the king so busy. He could leave his library, stroll from his castle to marketplace or forest. He saw that the consequences of chance in his country weren't always fortu-itous. Leaving the placement of a lookout tower to a coin toss had landed it in deep water, and, after weights and measures were made serendipitous, nothing ever fit right. But in their blowsy garments, the people themselves became less rigid. Im-perfection opened whole worlds to them: The underwater lookout tower became an aquarium. No longer beholden to the unalterable authority of history, folks were content to live, with their gambles and their mistakes, in the present. The king ob-served with approval, and perceived with relief that, for all in-tents and purposes, he was obsolete.

He traveled abroad. He saw countries led by tyrants whose uninterrupted rule entailed cauterizing subjects' tongues at birth, and countries managed by committees that maintained order by conscripting citizens in inconsequential meetings, leaving no time for mischief.

As a king, he was received everywhere with the respect cus-tomary for a visiting head of state, but the monarchs he met were puzzled by his abdication to circumstance. When the ser-vant he brought got homesick, the king sent him back to wife and children. When his slippers wore out, he went barefoot. Gradually, his robes tattered. His beard grew unkempt. Look-ing less like a sage than a madman, he wandered without direc-tion. He crossed his own path often, yet the landscape seemed to him more foreign with each passage. He saw fields sown with pebbles, irrigation channels running in spirals, houses with dozens of doors yet no windows.

Then one dusk, seeking a place to rest, he stepped out of the wilderness into a garden of storybook opulence. The ground was quilted with layer upon layer of exotic flowers, while overhead the trees were ornamented by the plumages of a thousand roosting birds. Easing himself into the vegetation, His Majesty slept more easily that evening than he ever had in his own castle.

At dawn, the king found a girl peering down at him. Her gown appeared to be an outgrowth of the garden, as if she'd been waiting for him there all season while a lily blossomed around her lissome figure. Her auburn hair was pinned up with one variegated feather. Yet it was her emerald eyes that he noticed most: He was sure he'd gazed into them before, in a palace somewhere.

He told her that he was a king, and asked if she was a princess. She asked if he cared for some breakfast. When he didn't answer, the girl guided him to a gazebo. In a crystal bowl, she tossed him a salad of white rose petals dressed in fresh dew.

— Where am I? Who are you? Have I stepped into a fairy tale?

— There's no such thing, Your Majesty. Don't you know? You're in your own country.

He scrutinized her more closely. He was sure she wasn't of the local gentry. Then he realized why her eyes were familiar: They were steeped in the same green as his dice.

— Will you marry me?

— What for?

— That's what girls do when kings offer.

— I'm content here by myself.

— Alone? You might be happier in my palace.

— I gambled once. It was enough.

— At least give me a chance?

— A gamble is only as good as the wager, Your Majesty. With all due respect, your kingdom is a slum. Tend to it. Make me want to leave this retreat.

As the girl walked away, a bird flew down and plucked the feather from her head. Her hair fell past her shoulders in a peasant's double braid.

· · ·

The king had to rouse his sentries from their beds to un-bolt his palace gate, as they'd ceased keeping regular hours. What did His Majesty expect, when time had stopped on the royal clock? Nobody knew what day or month it was anymore: Some subjects greeted the king as if they'd seen him moments before, others as if he'd been gone for years. He himself wasn't sure how long it had been, but he guessed he'd been absent quite a while, since nothing was as he recalled. Workshops were abandoned, or used as gambling dens, where, for want of cash, promises were wagered and threats exchanged. All anybody had to eat were wild radishes and blackberries. Uncleared in eons, the forest floor was a resting place for bodies that folks hadn't bothered to bury, alphabetically or otherwise. And in the palace library the ancient books crumbled as the king's hands trembled, littering the floor with words arranged by chance. When he knelt down, they didn't make sense. He couldn't find a trace that he understood: History couldn't be recovered. He resolved to take greater care in the future.

Then he set about trying to fix the present. He implored his subjects to consider what they'd given up to chance, not only in daily housekeeping, but also in sense of purpose.

Those who could be bothered to put down their dice ar-gued with him. What was the point in living, they demanded, when all possibilities had already been worked out for them, anticipated in books written before they were born? Once he'd granted them free will, they insisted, he couldn't usurp it.

Really he couldn't make them do anything at all. So he re-turned to his castle, and resumed his post without his subjects. He reviewed laws and made plans. And gradually, seeing him in the palace every day, simply knowing he was there because he'd chosen to be, others began to wonder whether surrendering their lives entirely to games of chance was so freeing.

One by one, they returned to work. Farmers farmed.

Millers milled. Tradesmen began setting up in the marketplace again. Taxes were collected. The palace clock was reset and the calendar recast. Time resumed. But if its form was the same, its function was different: descriptive rather than prescriptive. Folks worked from experience with the seasons, choosing which crops to plant and when, yet rolled with the consequences of their decisions. They learned to gamble wisely, took their chances seriously.

Busier than ever, helping his subjects see the potential of each new situation they faced, the king staked all he still had on his little province. And so it happened that, one afternoon, while consulting his library on a matter of crop rotation—the books made much more sense when he saw apparently contradictory rules as alternate suggestions—he heard a clamor in the streets as if some unforeseen jackpot had been hit. He mounted a spiral of stairs to the palace observation post. The sentry murmured the word *princess* and pointed at a lone auburn-haired figure on horseback. She looked up. He dropped to his knees and extended a hand. Her whispered assent, a simple yes, was picked up by the voices of those nearest to her on the road, carried by folks around them, radiating in every direction until it spoke to everyone in the kingdom.

The girl was married in her lily gown. Around her neck shimmered countless diamonds as small as dewdrops. Folks were awed by her fortune—a king's ransom—which became part of the crown when His Majesty made her his queen. And, for her part, she found herself so much happier than she'd been alone, so much more fulfilled, that she soon was pregnant.

Many years later, Gimmel the gambler passed through the region again. He had to ask the name of the country, for he didn't recognize it. No longer did the kingdom resemble a widow's vegetable garden. Houses of every color and shape stretched across the landscape. Folks shouted and bartered in the market, strolling around as if they owned the place. He didn't need to show them how to play dice. In fact, they taught him a new game, called craps.

Some of the young men laughed at Gimmel because he didn't know the latest casino lingo. They made fun of his missing eye and fingers, his penny-ante wagers, his cheap old dice that seemed never to roll his number. But an elderly farmer passing through the market recognized him, and told the boys that Gimmel had invented gambling. While that wasn't strictly accurate, the impression it made was dramatic. They brought him food and wine, and called him Father, as if he'd founded a religion.

It wasn't long before the king heard that such blasphemies were being spoken in his domain. He ordered the pretender captured and brought to him. The guards converged on the marketplace from every direction. They shackled Gimmel in irons. The king watched while they delivered him. The accused reached out a two-fingered hand.

— Gimmel?

— Your Majesty?

Waving away the shackles, the king offered the gambler a suite of rooms. He ordered a bath drawn.

For hours, a clutch of servants washed and scrubbed Gimmel. The water clotted into mud. A second bath was prepared, and then a third. Always more dirt. The servants wondered whether the gambler might erode to nothing, but no matter how many miles of mountain and valley they washed away, the man always looked like muck. They gave up. They put him back in his burlap frock, and showed him to the chamber where the royal family dined.

His Majesty was already there, seated at a small table set for four. He wore his longest cerulean robe, fringed in silver to match his great fronds of beard. The queen was opposite him, and, across from Gimmel, their sixteen-year-old girl. The princess wore her auburn hair in peasant braids, a style she'd learned from her mother, whose younger figure hers conjured like a reflection in fresh water. The gambler winced when he saw her.

— She has eyes the color of the dice you once gave me, Gimmel. Just like her mother. Now tell me, what did you do with all the money I lost to you that day?

— I gambled everything away.

— That must have taken a while.

— No, not at all.

The meal was served. The soup was made from blackberries and radishes, which, long after farmers had begun to grow a full range of crops again, were found in fact to be a tasty combination. After that, there was game hunted in the forest, and a salad of sweet white flowers raised by the princess. The wine was sweet as well, and, after a third glass, the gambler was enticed by His Majesty to tell what had become of the money. He glanced again at the princess—who'd taken to unknotting and reknitting her auburn braids in order to avoid his crooked cyclops gaze—and then at the aged queen herself. At last he said that his fortunes had turned less than an hour's journey from the palace.

One of the wagons carrying his treasure hit a rut (he told the king), and while he labored to get it out, a peasant woman came over and asked what he was carrying. He said the cart held half a fortune, and the rest was in the other one. Since she wouldn't believe him, he let her look beneath the covering, and told her where his bounty came from. Putting up her auburn braids, she tried on a diamond tiara. The fit was perfect. She sighed and declared that she was meant to be a princess.

Gimmel had to agree. So that she wouldn't leave, he offered to share his fortune.

— And what do I have to do?

— Be my companion.

She looked him over, and shuddered. She exclaimed he was uglier than a fairy-tale frog. She said that if he wanted the chance to wed her, he'd have to gamble everything he had.

Without a moment's hesitation, the gambler reached into his tobacco pouch. The girl set her emerald eyes on his wooden dice. She chose the number seven for luck. Gimmel chose two, the only number that mattered anymore.

They each took a die. She threw hers with eagerness. It came up one. His hand trembled, his will to win shaking, for the first time, the thrill of gambling. His die dropped. He looked. He'd rolled a royal six—and lost his chance to leap, so to speak, from frog to prince.

The girl kissed him anyway, once, on the lips. Nothing changed.

When Gimmel's tale was through, the king wanted to know why he'd consented to bet his whole fortune instead of just one cart.

— Surely no peasant could be worth all that.

— She bet everything, Your Majesty. How could I not do the same?

— And what happened to this fortunate young girl? Why haven't I heard of her, if she lives so near?

— You have. You married her.

The king looked at his wife. For a moment, under the sparkling tiara of chandelier light, her gray hairs seemed to tinge auburn. Her green eyes settled on him. His Majesty saw that the gambler spoke the truth.

To show his gratitude, the king proposed that Gimmel take his daughter for a wife. The princess shrieked, but before she could escape the old frog, he declined. He left the palace that night, carrying only his wooden dice. Happily ever after might be fit for a king, but such was not a fate given to a gambler.

DALET THE THIEF

Dalet was a thief. He'd learned to be a thief from his father, who'd apprenticed under his father's father, once upon a time: Thievery had been the family business for as long as anyone could remember. In his town, Dalet was the only thief, just as there was one family that produced coopers, while another raised each generation's butcher.

Of course every town needs a thief, and for forty years Dalet's father had fulfilled that role admirably well. The old man would filch the baker's batter spoon, or swipe the shoemaker's leather apron, and, later the same day, the baker or shoemaker would come to his door to take back spoon or apron in exchange for a couple of coppers. Dalet's family had lived on that money. They'd never been wealthy, but they got by respectably, and when Dalet's father died, a widower of fifty, he had a wooden casket at a funeral attended by everybody.

On the whole, the village was prosperous by then. What could go wrong? Because Dalet's family was always to blame, nothing was ever missing for long. Nobody ever lost money or time. Folks spent their surplus on luxuries: gilded candlesticks and crystal goblets and gemstones for their unwed daughters.

Tailors and tinkers threw lavish suppers simply so their neighbors could admire a serving platter or a saltcellar or some embroidered table linen. Market day became a pageant of mass affluence, and collective envy.

In at least one respect, Dalet was not a good thief. Given the vast wealth around him, he should swiftly have become rich. But Dalet lacked ambition. Only when he had to, would he take the shoemaker's leather apron, and then he'd wait patiently for days before anyone would notice that it was gone. The village elders were worried about his behavior, concerned for the natural order. They summoned him to the town square.

— Why do you neglect your work, Dalet? Your father didn't teach you its value?

— I stole something last week. I took Avram the baker's batter spoon.

— Again?

— Why not?

— Avram has more batter spoons than he can remember. He buys so many, carved from mahogany and cherry, that he can't be bothered to bake a batch of bread. All he does is spend money. One day he orders a pair of boots, the next day it's a set of horses, while the batter sits in a vat and rots.

— I should steal a better spoon, then?

—One day you'll want to marry, Dalet. You'll have to provide for a family. You won't be able to survive on batter spoons alone.

—I've also stolen Dov the shoemaker's leather apron.

—Dov's too busy chasing after Zev the carpenter about building a new home even to cobble Avram's new boots for him. Why should he care if you take his smock? Listen, Dalet. Like any tradesman, a thief has to keep up with the times. You've got to steal what people need. Otherwise someone else might. And a village with more than one thief is more cursed than a country with two kings.

. . .

When Dalet got home that evening, he took the baker's batter spoon from behind the stove. The spoon was over a century old, so often stolen by his family, over so many generations, that it was practically an heirloom. He knew its contour better than the shape of his own crooked face. It was beautiful to him like a woman. A living thing. A companion. Yet on that night, as darkness deepened around him, he saw that he was all alone.

He put on his father's black cloak. Tradition held that the garment made him invisible to honest people, though he'd never told a lie and yet could plainly see himself. Still, Dalet was not one to question tradition, and he'd nothing else to keep him warm. He grasped the spoon and shut his door.

Dalet lived in a decrepit shack outside the town. The walk to the baker's house took ten minutes under a full moon, and at least half an hour on a night as black as this. He passed the stables, followed by the town square, where Shlomo the watchman strolled past without a greeting. Guided by the light cast from Shlomo's lantern, Dalet entered Avram's home through the unlocked front door.

The family was asleep, all except the youngest daughter. Comely little Riva wore a slip of white lace, and several rings on slender adolescent fingers. She emerged from the larder, nibbling on a crust. Though drenched in honey, the bread was crummy, inevitably stale since the village imported baked goods from the city. She glanced at Dalet's invisible cloak, and then his crooked face. Setting down the candle that she carried, she met his luminous eyes.

— What are you doing here?

— I'm returning your father's spoon.

— Why? No one wants it.

— I know. I'm supposed to steal stuff that people care about.

— People care about stars. If you wish on them, they twinkle.

— I can't filch stars. I'm afraid of heights.

— How about jewels? Everyone wants those. It's why they sparkle.

— Do you mean you can actually see what people desire?

— Don't you know, Dalet? Look around you.

Tossing the old spoon into the larder behind some bags of grain, she blew out the candle. Even in the darkness, Dalet saw her smile. He trembled, yet before he could extend a hand, she'd shuffled down a corridor. As her footsteps drifted off, the room faded black.

Standing in the dark, Dalet reckoned: Stars twinkled and jewels sparkled and when a girl was wed, when her groom met her at the altar, she had to hide behind a veil for fear of blinding him. Desire burned in everything, sometimes less, sometimes more, kindled by the beholder. But while children could perceive that flame plainly, adults felt it only indirectly, as the heat of envy, unless—

Haltingly, Dalet followed the hallway in the direction that the girl had gone, sensing a dim light ahead of him. As he approached, he whispered Riva's name. No response. His hand touched the leg of a table, where she'd set out her rings for him. He left them. He continued to wander, exploring the constellation of desire.

The following room revealed more. Dalet discerned rows of dishes, ranks of silverware. He counted a dozen blown-glass goblets, each rim aglow like a small halo. Yet nothing dazzled like what he sensed below. He stretched out his hand, found that he had to open a cabinet, where something precious had been concealed behind piles of linen.

Smaller than he'd imagined, but burning more fiercely than he'd have believed: a decanter cut from a single rock crystal. Did it hold hellfire? Dalet checked that the stopper was tight, and, embracing his lot in life, made his escape.

Outside, the decanter shone like a lantern, illuminating his way. Moths came to him, washing their dank wings in the light, wishing to awaken as butterflies. Dalet rested in the town square to give them time, though he reckoned that the chances of metamorphosis were slim. More moths gathered. There must have been a hundred by the time Shlomo the watchman made his hourly round. Old Shlomo loathed moths, for he'd heard that they carried omens from dusk to dawn. He swatted and shouted until all were gone. Then he walked on, leaving Dalet by himself again, unnoticed in the decanter's spectral glow.

By sunrise, everyone in the baker's household was awake: his wife, his two sons, and all but his youngest daughter. Avram sent his eldest girl, twenty-four-year-old Tamar, to wake her.

— Don't you know what day it is, Riva?

— Tell me later. I don't care.

— Tonight is Papa's banquet. We have to prepare. Where are your rings, Riva?

— I left them on a table somewhere. I told you, I don't care.

Tamar left her to tell their father of Riva's latest mischief. She found Avram kneeling on the floor, digging linen out of a cabinet, cursing each rag as if it were a demon. His wife stood behind him, gathering up the fabric, refolding each piece. Tamar wanted to know what was wrong, but her mother just shrugged and put her to work on a heap of napkins.

Avram reached the back of the cabinet. Nothing there. He tore out the shelving. He stood up and lifted the thing. He shook it, and hurled it out the door.

What was the matter? his whole family asked him, and how could he answer? The crystal decanter had been his secret, cut at the utmost expense in a foreign country for this banquet. A secret that would surprise everybody: His neighbors would forever be put in their place, a feat for which his wife and children would eternally admire—and, yes, envy—him. He shook his head, and sought out Shlomo the watchman.

Shlomo slept during the day in an underground hut. Over the years, night had seeped into his eyes, where it had pooled until all he had were two black pupils. He couldn't see in daylight, naturally, but after dark he often compensated by perceiving more than was actually there. Avram stomped on his hatch until Shlomo awoke and let him crawl under. The baker made sure no one else was there. He lowered his voice. He asked whether the watchman had seen anything suspect the previous evening.

— As a matter of fact, I did.

— I knew it.

— The moths were out.

— What?

— Hundreds of them.

— Moths?

— Moths carry omens, Avram. They carry omens from dusk to dawn.

— I don't care about that. It's not what I'm talking about.

— You've never seen moths like these.

— What I want to know is if you saw a person, a human being, breaking into my house, or getting away carrying . . .

— . . . An omen?

— No, Shlomo. A cut-crystal decanter.

— Don't be silly. Why would anybody do that around here?

Avram didn't have an answer. The only conceivable reason would be to ruin him, yet ever since he'd bought his horses, the village had shown him nothing but deference. He went home. He interrogated his family. He demanded to know if they'd moved anything without his permission. He wouldn't say what was gone. Nevertheless, he made them search the house and bring him all they found.

The place was loaded with treasures, fashioned of gold and lapis, silk and tortoiseshell. Avram had forgotten how much he had. But each time his wife or children came to him, he shook his head. It got late. In two hours, guests would arrive for the banquet. Tamar reminded her father that she and her sisters had to dress and braid one another's hair. He nodded. They went away, all but Riva.

— Have you gone to Dalet the thief, Papa?

— I spoke to Shlomo.

— But if a thief wears his cloak . . .

— Don't be foolish. Poor Dalet takes my worthless batter spoon . . .

— It's in the larder.

— Why didn't you bring it to me before?

— If it's worthless, why would you care?

Avram saw that his spoon was where his daughter said, which was odd: By his reckoning, the spoon had been gone for ages, not worth its customary two-penny ransom. Avram was a modern man—as his wealth well proved—and knew that an object couldn't simultaneously be in Dalet's possession and in his own hands. He went to investigate.

Dalet was at home in his shack. He hadn't left since he awoke, too entranced by the decanter even to let his eyes wander. He sat and watched desire churn inside, quickening in morning torment, lengthening into afternoon longing. He learned the language of want. He knew that Avram was coming even before the baker left his own house.

He opened the door as Avram approached. They met on the road. Deprived of the chance to ambush Dalet, Avram decided to trick him. He took two pennies from his purse and dropped them in the thief's hand.

— I'm here to take back my batter spoon.

— You already have it.

— Isn't it your job to filch it?

— Not anymore. My job is to steal people's needs.

Avram didn't understand what the village thief meant. But he knew perfectly well, as Dalet invited him inside, that the decanter on the table was the one he'd bought for his banquet. He said so. Dalet agreed. Avram grew large with rage: How could the thief pilfer it? Dalet reiterated what he'd been told by the town elders.

Avram couldn't argue with them, for they were shortly to be his guests. So he took a seat and reached again inside his purse. He hadn't any more coppers. He withdrew a fat gulden, and set it on the table between them.

The gold glowed pure greed, but what match was that for the blaze of Avram's desperation? One gulden was the same as another: Their glimmer was shared. Dalet could barely even see the coin in the decanter's glare. He declined the offer.

Avram added another gulden, and then several more. At last he emptied his purse. But it was like casting stars into sunlight. Poor Avram, his reckoning was all wrong: In matters of desire, no quantity is greater than one.

— How much do you want, Dalet? Is my gold not enough? Do you want my silk? My lapis? My daughter Tamar? I'll go get her. She won't complain. My banquet will be your wedding.

Dalet had often seen Tamar in the marketplace. She was built tall and stiff like a post, fenced in her own crossed arms. Though he didn't wear his invisibility cloak in the daytime, she'd never acknowledged him, and, while he was accustomed to being overlooked, he had trouble imagining how he'd fulfill his marital duties without her participation, whether a woman could conceive children without even noticing that she had a husband. Then Dalet's thoughts returned to little Riva. He recalled how she'd smiled at him. His memory flared anew with her unbridled light, overwhelming the decanter's stoppered glow. Dalet put both hands on the table.

— I'd like Riva.

— Riva is my youngest.

— I want to marry her. You can have the decanter.

— I can't give away my daughters out of order, Dalet. Tamar is already twenty-four, and Riva . . . My eldest must be married first. You know that's the way of the world. Would you have me break the law?

The thief sighed. His breath made the decanter shimmer, a sympathetic quivering of the desire pent up within. In that light, he saw the tumble of Riva's auburn hair, the moisture in her copper eyes, the downturn of her mouth as she gnawed on a stale crust. He sighed again, and, wishing for what she might want, mumbled the words *fresh bread.*

— What did you say?

— I'll return the decanter if you'll bake some challah.

— How about a wagonload of whole-grain import? It's only three days old, a week at most.

— No, Avram. I want it made here, by you.

— I haven't baked in ages, Dalet.

— I'll return your decanter when you do.

By the time Avram got home, Dov the shoemaker and Zev the carpenter were already at his banquet, as were the tailor and the cooper and the butcher. If he'd bartered with senseless Dalet any longer, he wouldn't have been on hand to greet Yehudah the mayor and his wife, Esther, his coveted guests of honor. More people came, and on each new face the baker looked to find the disappointment that he himself felt—that he felt toward himself—for not having a cut-crystal decanter on the table. But they couldn't even see where it would have gone: Not knowing of it, his wife had left no place for it. To everybody but Avram, the decanter didn't exist.

They toasted him. They praised the beauty of his wife and daughters. They complimented the mutton he served them and admired the plates on which it was served. Avram tried to stop them, to object that nothing could compare to his decanter, but they wouldn't let him. Dov praised his silk. Zev complimented his tortoiseshell. Yehudah admired how his money shimmered like jewelry. But the toasts weren't celebratory; they sounded like an inventory. And if folks could make such a fuss about things so obviously inferior to his decanter, Avram knew their envy didn't add up to much.

At last they left, just hours before the coming of dawn. His family went to bed. Avram didn't sleep, though. He slipped down the cellar stairs to fetch a load of wood. He hauled it next door, where his stone ovens were, and built a fire. When he turned around, he found little Riva there, still draped in satin, hair braided with amber. She was carrying his batter spoon.

— Why wasn't Dalet at the banquet tonight?

— Because he's a thief, Riva.

— He has luminous eyes.

— He's got a crooked face.

— That may be, but he's never told a lie.

Avram stared at his daughter for a while, trying to discern whether the thief had gone ahead and seduced her without his permission. However, he saw no abrasions, none of the blunders that a man might leave in the night, and he attributed her own fervid state to his good wine. He stooped to gather flour and water. He mixed his batter in a great vat. He kneaded it. Riva went to sleep in the corner. He covered the dough with a white shroud. He wrapped his daughter's shawl around her febrile shoulders, and carried her to bed.

The town awoke to a scent as strangely familiar as the touch of a lost lover. Husbands and wives whispered to each other, but it wasn't gossip about the banquet. All they said was: *fresh bread.* They dressed in a hurry, no time for jewels and finery. They crowded around the bakery.

Avram opened the door to get away from the heat of his oven. The people in the street engulfed him. They wanted to know when the bread would be ready. They jangled their money.

Avram sold them all the challah he had, all but the loaf he'd set aside for the thief. Those who came late wanted to buy that. He was offered a gulden, five, ten. He was barricaded by a veritable auction, and might have been detained all day had he not promised to bake a bigger batch the following morning.

Concealing the loaf under a silk swathe, he went at last to see Dalet. Though he didn't say where he was going, little Riva followed him down the road, and refused to turn around.

— You can't come with me. What do you want?

— Why isn't the bread you baked for us?

— It's ransom. You wouldn't understand.

— Dalet must have stolen something that you love very much.

Recalling his decanter, Avram couldn't bear to be detained by his daughter's banter any longer. He permitted her to accompany him if she promised not to talk to the thief, and to shun his crooked gaze.

They entered Dalet's hovel together. Accustomed to hardwood luxury, Riva was shocked by the conditions in Dalet's shack, scarcely the size of Avram's pantry, a slum of rot and rust, in which the thief sat, rough and unwashed. Heeding her father's orders, she didn't say hello, and stared at Dalet's ruined shoes while her father addressed him, unwrapping the swaddling, unveiling the precious loaf.

Dalet cradled his hands around the warm heft. He split off a braid, and gave it to Riva. Then he handed a portion to the baker and took a piece for himself. Seated around his hobbled table, they ate together.

At last Dalet stood. He retrieved the decanter from behind some rubbish—stolen goods ages abandoned—and handed it to the baker. The light within lifted as Avram held it out for the admiration of his daughter.

She shrugged and asked if she could have more challah. The glow dissipated. Avram stepped outside and held the crystal to the sun to see why it no longer seemed so spectacular. As she watched him turn it, Riva found the bread in her hands replenished. Filling her mouth, she furtively glanced at the thief. In the combined light of their eyes, the decanter seemed to vanish.

The following night, Avram brought the decanter to Dov the shoemaker as a gift. Dov had been to the bakery that morning to buy bread for the evening's feast, a bacchanal to rival Avram's own banquet. The shoemaker had placed his order with the pomp of a prince. But in the dozen hours that had passed, he'd collapsed. He absently set the decanter in a corner. Avram was too hungry for a taste of his own bread to wonder what had overcome the shoemaker. Only little Riva saw how Dov's gaze dropped, from everyone whose eyes met his, to the floor.

His rug was gone: Dalet had stolen the carpet Dov was said to have purchased from a dybbuk. It had cost a fortune, but how do you bargain with a demon? And, after all, people didn't see such a rug every day. The colors weren't earthly: none of the usual mud and silt. Woven from the purple and gold that embellish dreams, it set hopes at folks' feet.

Girls ached to dance with Dov. He could have carried any one away to bed or altar in a single leap. He declined. Other men caught them when they swooned, and spun them around as if—who needs a dybbuk's carpet?—there weren't any gravity.

Dov slept in his shop that night, to escape the oppressive festivity of his bacchanal. And in the morning, he took up the old boots on his bench: Dalet's shoes, toe-holed and hob-nailed, fixed ad hoc over the years by anyone with a hammer, yet somehow still possessed of the pedestrian integrity that Dov had learned from his father. He glanced at his own boots, purchased prefabricated from the peddler who lately came to town four times a year, selling chic city shoes, styled in filigree and leaf, that aged a lifetime in a season. Disposable footwear: Everyone but Dalet had bought into that. When the thief had refused, the previous afternoon, to return Dov's dybbuk carpet for cash—when Dalet had instead insisted that the shoemaker resole his boots—Dov had offered him enough new shoes to last a decade. But, as the whole town knew, Dalet was obtuse: He refused to be wealthy like everybody else. What was Dov to do? He tied on his smock and got to work.

Craftsmen, naturally, have standards: A good pair of soles deserves heels at least their equal, and the bottom of a shoe shouldn't make a mockery of the top. Dov labored at his bench all day long, hunched and pinched, remaking each piece of those old clodhoppers, replacing every stretch of leather, each iron fitting. Folks pounded at his door, but he mistook it for the echo of his mallet. They called to him through the window, but he thought it was the whine of his grindstone. Only after his job was done did he notice that the day was gone.

Dov lit a lantern and slung Dalet's boots over his shoulder. He opened his door. Nobody was outside anymore—but everyone's shoes were. The line of footwear stood unbroken from Dov's shop to the town square. Dov picked up the first pair. He recognized from the pitch of the arch that he'd made them for

Zev the carpenter. They required new straps. The next pair in line needed to be reheeled, and, on those after that, the leather had cracked.

On his way to the thief's hovel, Dov worked over those shoes in his head. He weighed what size nails he'd need, and followed the thread of each anticipated suture over hill and through pasture to Dalet's door. He stepped inside. He seated the thief, and, down on his knees, adjusted the boots to fit Dalet's feet.

— Come to me if they hurt.

— Let me fetch your carpet.

— Another day. I have too much work.

The following morning, Dov fixed Zev's shoes, and brought them to him in the afternoon. Zev looked upset.

— Is the stitching too tight?

— The gems I set aside to pay you with, they were stolen last night.

— What would I do with a pile of rocks? I need you to build some shelves in my shop.

Who can say what makes a village change its ways? Of course, the thief was the first to see a difference. On market day, desire no longer radiated, as if an act of nature, from the town square. And if Dalet broke into the home of the cooper or the butcher, he often couldn't distinguish one luxury from another: Objects didn't quite lose their luster, but each gave a light so similar to the others that they might as well have been a line of yahrzeits. For a time, Dalet didn't know what to steal. The tailor's porcelain figurines? An emerald brooch from the tinker's wife? Why bother? Folks didn't care a farthing for such baubles anymore.

The treasures began to stockpile in Dalet's hovel. He foisted what he could on itinerant beggars, but how many candlesticks and goblets could he expect them to haul? Furniture gridlocked his floor, paintings plastered his walls, and if he burdened his bed with another piece of linen, he'd be lying on the ceiling.

He couldn't sleep. Wrapped in his cloak, he wandered the night. He tried to chat with Shlomo the watchman, to pass the time in conversation, but, whenever Dalet spoke, Shlomo acted as if his were the voice of an apparition: The watchman dropped his lantern and fled. So listless Dalet talked to the moths. They appreciated his company as long as he stood by Shlomo's lamp. He gave them voice lessons, lest they think that only butterflies could be pretty. And he told them about his beloved Riva, whose beauty he beheld without either sight or sound.

On that matter, they didn't appear convinced. All his life, the thief had stolen people's needs, and folks hadn't been content—had they?—merely to possess memories. If Dalet really needed Riva, if he truly loved her, the moths reasoned with beating wings, he'd quit meddling in other people's desires. He'd go to Avram's house and steal her.

Lacking an education, Dalet couldn't argue with them. He buttoned his invisibility cloak, and strode over to Avram's home. He climbed the stairs, and found Riva's room.

She lay uncovered atop a feather bed, linen tangled at her ankles and blankets rumpled on the carpet. In her sleep she'd unlaced her slip. The loose ribbons dangled from the fingers of two little hands resting on new breasts beneath flush nipples. Dalet knelt to lift her, so much lighter than the marble nymph he'd pilfered from Yehudah's garden the night before. The statue now rested in his hovel, numb to desire. Riva, though, she wasn't stone sculpture. She wasn't a rug or a decanter.

The moths had been mistaken. What Dalet wanted couldn't be stolen; love had to be given.

A breeze ruffled Riva's curtains. She shivered in her sleep. Dalet removed his invisibility cloak and tucked it around her shoulders and hips and thighs and feet. Then he left her, shutting the door and shuffling home alone.

In the morning, Riva's sisters went to wake her, to work in the bakery with their father. All they found in her bed was an empty slip. They picked up her blankets. They shook out her sheets. Carrying her linens in their arms, they hurried to Avram.

He stood at the door to his bakery, staring into an overcast sky. They told him that Riva was missing. They held out the bedding. Avram raised a hand, as if he'd already guessed. One by one they stopped talking, following his eyes: The storm clouds ahead looked luminous.

All over town, folks stepped out of their shops to squint at the shock of light on the horizon, showering radiance across the sunless sky.

— Is that Dalet's hovel?

— Impossible. His shack is too small.

Yet even those who expressed doubt began to walk toward the light. They followed the road brightening toward Dalet's house. As they turned the final bend, the brilliance was too much. Folks covered their faces.

Only Avram didn't, searing open eyes looking for his daughter until, at the crux of the blaze, he saw spreading shadow. It unfurled like a cloak, and wrapped around an emerging double filament. The sky fell black.

. . .

The pyrotechnics of desire left the house and village un-blemished. Gradually Avram recovered his eyesight. For many weeks, people searched for Riva and Dalet. Plank by plank, they dismantled his hovel. They found only trifles.

Yet the couple, though never again seen, did not abandon them. Periodically a loaf of bread would be missing from a batch, or a supply of wood would come up short. Folks accepted these losses. Any imbalance was attributed to the hidden lovers. Even as years passed, and their faces were forgotten, their names were murmured to bless, and mend, any inade-quacy. The town no longer had a thief, and no longer needed one.

HEYH THE CLOWN

When Heyh was a small girl, her mother traded her to the circus for a sack of potatoes. That was the exchange rate in those days—just price for a child her size—half the value of a laborer, and twice that of a cadaver.

Only in this particular case, the circus made a mistake: Whereas most children are natural acrobats, suggestibly flexible, Heyh was a klutz. In fact, none of the troupe had ever seen a human being so helplessly clumsy. Romping around on feet broad enough to carry a grown man, she knocked over scenery and props, or stumbled on imperceptible obstacles: faded shadows, diminished echoes. When that happened, she tried to catch herself with hands large enough to paddle a boat. Were she not so squat, she might have been seriously hurt.

Compared to Heyh, a sack of potatoes had ballerina grace. Yet, what coordination her body lacked, she compensated for in the mobility of her face. She'd wide blue eyes and full red lips that captured her emotions and projected them farther than— poor girl, she also had an astigmatism—she could possibly observe. The other newly purchased children made fun of Heyh, just to see her cry. They mimicked her gait, walked into imaginary walls and slipped on make-believe banana peels, but she didn't perceive that they were mocking her. So whenever she stepped out from under the tent where the troupe lived and practiced together in winter, her companions beat the tears out of her with fists.

The adults beat her as well, but only as a disciplinary measure when she fell off the tightrope or missed the trapeze. It was part of her training, as was lobbing rocks at her to encourage agility. None of which improved her performance. Any ordinary guild would have given up on Heyh. A circus, however, is a family, and, if they couldn't sell her by the time the weather turned warm and the troupe began to travel and perform, they'd find some role for her to play.

Because Heyh had such ample hands, Iser the juggler tried to teach her his skills with sticks and balls. To her unfocused eyes, however, the objects traveled as a blur, and she was at a loss to catch them when they fell from the air. Nor did her massive feet help her to stand on the back of a galloping horse like Shimmel the acrobat did in his opening act; affronted to be saddled with such an awkward load, the animals all threw her to the ground. Schprintze the contortionist refused to waste time on a girl whose movements were so disjointed, and Teyvel the sword-swallower said she was too short to fit a saber all the way down her throat. By springtime, all the other children had acts of their own: Koppel was a fire walker, Fishke did some sleight-of-hand, the sisters Hodel and Hinde were tumblers, and Glukel had paired up with Iser as the target in his new knife-throwing routine. Only little Heyh still couldn't do anything.

They put her onstage anyway. In the first town, they set her on a trapeze suspended from an oak tree. As the applause for Hodel and Hinde's acrobatic tussle climaxed, Shimmel shoved Heyh from her perch. She passed over the crowd in a perfect arc of flight, but, when her hands released at the peak, she failed to catch the beam with her feet. The shame cast across her face as she hit the side of the barn made Shimmel shut his eyes in pain. The crowd, though, wasn't the least bit upset by her act, loudly laughing at her as she crawled behind a rock and cried. People couldn't take their eyes off the unfortunate girl. They scarcely noticed Teyvel when he took the stage and swallowed a five-foot-long rapier while standing in a ring of fire.

In the next town, Shimmel hoisted Heyh onto the tightrope as Hodel and Hinde exited the stage, to loud cheers, with a double-headed backflip. The high wire was strung above a river. Heyh walked toe-to-heel like she'd been taught, smiling at her audience far below. As she got to the center, though, she felt the rope shivering in the breeze. Her knees started to tremble. The line began to shake. Her legs struggled to compensate. The wire wriggled faster, sending giggles through the crowd below her. She looked down. She remembered she couldn't swim. She tried to back up, misjudged the length of her foot. Down she went. She hit the water belly-first, and sank.

It was Shimmel who fetched her. As he pulled her to the surface, she heard folks' jeers, even heartier than on the day before. She didn't ever want to perform again. She wished that she had drowned.

Teyvel wished that she'd died as well when, for the second day in a row, nobody paid attention to his act after her collapse, and Hodel and Hinde were getting impatient about how their routine was forgotten by the time Heyh's was finished. But most of the troupe was starting to recognize her value: As much as folks enjoyed being elevated by feats they could never physically achieve, they also sought the affirmation of watching someone fail more dramatically than they'd ever done. They needed a buffoon, a slapstick scapegoat to comically relieve them of their own inadequacies. Heyh did it spectacularly.

As the season went on, Shimmel and Iser and Schprintze choreographed increasingly elaborate routines for her. They'd have her juggle fire on the tightrope, which would ignite when she dropped a flare, inflaming her clothing as she tumbled into the lake beneath her. Teyvel, meanwhile, made every effort, short of murder, to kill her. He set out his knives under her trapeze, or loosed Shimmel's horse while Heyh struggled to get out of a pond.

She no longer smiled for the crowd as her act began. She paled. Her tear ducts swelled, and still they ran dry by the end of each day. Hodel and Hinde each budded breasts that summer, and were promptly deflowered by Teyvel. Glukel grew pregnant with Iser's child. Shimmel and Schprintze had their annual fling. Koppel and Fishke started sharing the same bed. Everyone was wanted but Heyh. Everyone was loved and admired. She begged, day after day, to quit the circus, to be left on the side of the road.

— You're just getting good on the trapeze, Heyh. And think of your juggling.

— I can't do it. I can't do anything.

— The crowds love you.

— They like to make fun.

— You're too humble. You're imagining things. You're deluded, selfish, egotistical. You don't appreciate what we've done for you. You're trying to embarrass us. You can't understand how the audience needs you. You're not smart enough. Don't be a buffoon.

Upstaged by their verbal gymnastics, Heyh got back on the trapeze and redoubled her acrobatic efforts.

And, because of her, their circus swiftly became more popular. Stories of her foibles traveled farther and wider than the troupe ever had. Eager to see her high-wire humiliations, towns everywhere extended invitations to perform. Naturally they didn't care about the sword-swallowing or the fire-walking or sleight-of-hand, which could easily be seen locally. The others' routines gradually coalesced into a contrasting backdrop for

Heyh's act, an excuse to lay out all the scenery that tripped her up, and a means of making a good living at her expense. Even Hodel and Hinde stopped learning new tricks, preferring to compete for Teyvel's waning interest. The troupe locked Heyh in a cage, lest she try to run away, and spent all day counting money.

With each performance, she grew more reckless. At first the troupe thought that Shimmel was getting sloppy about the heights from which he pushed her trapeze or the vigor with which he shook her high wire. Then they thought it was Teyvel, still out to hurt her. At last they decided that it might be the effect of imprisonment in a cage day and night. Instead they tied her up in a potato sack.

The change had no perceptible effect. They gave up trying to understand Heyh, to figure out what would have been hideously clear had any of them bothered to look her in the face: Whether by rope or fire or knife, the girl wished to be dead. Of course she couldn't commit suicide, the buffoon. She was no more capable of killing herself than of doing anything else.

One day, word of Heyh's ill-fated stunts reached the big city. A small delegation went out into the country to watch her perform. Her hands and feet weren't as large as reported, and, to these strangers, she seemed neither comically ugly nor deformed. Yet they were not disappointed by her clumsiness. Indeed, these connoisseurs of human foibles and vice were positively elated to find in her a completely self-made failure, unsophisticated by liquor, unadulterated by sexual misadventure: Her buffoonery cast no aspersions on others' foolishness. Her comedy was universal. Everybody, even drunkards and perverts, could scorn her.

The alderman heading the delegation knew a smash hit when he saw one. He presented Shimmel with a contract, which the acrobat signed with a spatter of ink. Five nights in a theater chartered by the king, with box-office returns determined by equations too elaborate for the troupe to fathom, the complexity of which figured incalculable success. Folding the contract into his pocket and the delegation into his carriage, the alderman left to prepare for the circus's grand entrance.

The troupe passed through the city gate a couple of days later. When they asked people where they should go, folks answered, *Who are you?* When they said they were the circus, folks responded, *Which one?* They weren't sure what to reply, for they'd never thought to take a name, so they rode around looking for a theater chartered by the king.

Apparently the king of this country had chartered many things, and the troupe found his coat of arms painted on pubs and baths, brothels and gambling dens. Half a dozen times, they approached a theater, only to be told that circuses were passé, and sent to a competitor.

At last somebody they met had heard that an unknown country circus was coming to town. He helped them to find a broadside, and read it aloud. The poster announced the arrival, by special arrangement, of Heyh the Clown. Iser asked if his famous juggling act was advertised. The man shook his head. Teyvel's sword-swallowing? Schprintze's contortions? Fishke's sleight-of-hand? None of them. Then Heyh asked what *clown* meant. The man just laughed, as if she were fooling, and pointed the company toward a theater down an unmarked alley of stockyards and slaughterhouses.

The alderman was not there. The manager, a bruiser called Yankel, whose face looked to have been butchered, explained that those in the delegation were investors, quality folks hardly to be seen in a burlesque hall on that side of town.

So they guessed that the king wasn't going to be attending their performances, either, especially after Yankel took them inside the hall, which had a dirt floor and not a single chair. Nor was there a stage per se, just a chalk line at the center. There was no roof, only a stone wall enclosing a space the size and shape of a stable.

Yankel was anxious to set up: Their first performance would be that night, under limelight. He'd no time to discuss why Hodel and Hinde weren't named on the broadside, and he merely guffawed when Heyh asked him what a clown did.

He did, however, have a costume for her, brightly patterned. None of the troupe had ever seen a costume before, much less thought to wear one, and, for a short while after she put it on, they stood around, admiring. Then they remembered who she was, and their admiration distilled into envy, which could be dispelled only by providing outfits to everyone.

Folks lined up outside while the ropes went up. Since there was no barn for Heyh to hit when she flew off the trapeze, Yankel had some boards thrown against the wall. Since there was no lake in which to have her fall, he threw a bucket of water on the floor. Then he sold tickets for a penny apiece until he couldn't shove another body through the door.

Nobody paid much attention to the warm-up acts: They ignored Shimmel's hackneyed horseback acrobatics, shouted out the secrets to Fishke's slapdash magic, jeered Iser's slipshod knife-throwing for failing once to penetrate pregnant Glukel, and heckled Hodel and Hinde for stumbling through their girl-on-girl gymnastics without stripping off each other's clothing. Finally, from a limelit platform, Yankel announced through his megaphone the world-renowned Heyh the Clown.

Something unfathomable happened that night, from the moment Shimmel pushed her out on the trapeze: Her recklessness metastasized into confidence. She didn't miss the beam with her feet when she let go, and her hands were there for her as she swung full-circle. She got it that night, and the tightrope as well, from which she juggled fire without once letting her knees buckle.

That was not what folks wanted. After all, they lived in a city where you could see meaner feats for half a penny any day of the week. They'd paid good money to see Heyh stagger and trip, maybe even break her neck. But aside from the costume, there was nothing clownish about her. She was merely mediocre.

They called her a fraud, and pelted her with rotten potatoes. They cut the tightrope and broke the trapeze. Someone got hold of the limelight, spilling it onto the floor. The fire flared. Yankel fled with the money chest. Iser and Koppel scaled the wall. The rest of the troupe followed.

They ran through unfamiliar streets in their colored costumes, pursued by men and women wielding weapons fleeced from Teyvel's chest. Urchins abandoned their empty-handed gambling to join in the pursuit. If they couldn't afford a stage show, at least they could see this troupe of buffoons, stupid country clowns, chased down and beaten.

By midnight, the troupe was miles outside the city. By daylight, they were safe in the forest. All except pregnant Glukel. She was gone. Naturally they couldn't turn around and fetch her. All that could be done was to blame Heyh and move on.

— Why is it my fault?

— You got us chased out of town.

— I only did what I was supposed to do. I even did it right this time.

— Don't you understand, you ass? If you're a clown, right is wrong.

The troupe looked for work. But wherever they went, they were preceded by word of their big-city bust. Of their debacle, every detail was known, and suitably embellished for swift travel. Some folks claimed that Heyh was a charlatan, whose accidents were simulated, and that her big-city flop was a failure of nerve. Others, better-educated, said that she'd been planning her metropolitan debut since the beginning, that all along she'd been playing her audience for the fool, and not crashing that evening was her ultimate act of ridicule. Where Heyh the Clown was not mocked, she was loathed.

The circus ran out of money. They'd no equipment, no props, and, aside from Yankel's harlequin attire, no clothes. Another winter was coming. Cold and snow. And their whole company was no longer worth a sack of potatoes.

Now it happened that Schprintze's family was from a country at war. The trouble had begun there, several years before, through no human fault, but rather on account of an earthquake that had split the land. The schism was neither deep nor wide, and could easily have been filled, had people been able to agree on where the requisite stone should be quarried. But folks on the eastern side of the kingdom claimed that the gap lay to the west, while those on the western countered, following the same line of logic, that it lay to the east: In short, each side believed that responsibility fell to the other, and accused the other of divisiveness.

It was a matter that the king could have settled with a word. But the skirmish got no response from him, as if the quake had struck him dumb. For weeks and months, advisers tried to talk their young monarch out of his fugue, all the while secretly shuttling him between east and west lest either side lay claim to him, yet his silence was increasingly irrelevant as the scrimmage hardened into war.

Regional differences were found in every commonplace. Folks discovered idioms and accents. More ambitious militants raised armies on arguments of larger consequence: Who owned the water in the rivers or the rain clouds in the sky? Did the east withhold the sun in the morning, or was the west embezzling it at night? Such philosophical matters, usually minded by the crown, were abdicated to the generals, who agreed to disagree, and to blow each other's soldiers to smithereens.

This, then, is where the circus traveled in search of work. Schprintze was right in her prediction that the troupe's high-wire acrobatics would be a welcome distraction to troops who passed their lives hunkered down on the front line. Eager to boost battalion morale, generals were pleased to exchange provisions for entertainment, and soldiers simply needed something to lighten the mood while they killed.

Shrewdly taking neither side, the circus moved freely around the country, dazzling everybody. Armies provided the equipment—ropes to walk, clubs to juggle, swords to swallow—from their own arsenals. And, as for costumes, Teyvel cleverly had everyone in the troupe perform their superhuman feats in the uniform of the hosting battalion. All except for Heyh: She was pinned with the insignia of the opposing military.

Since the big-city calamity, she'd also been assigned a new role. No longer trusted on trapeze or tightrope, she was assigned to replace Glukel as Iser's human target.

She was awful at it. Unlike sweet Glukel, she couldn't keep still. Each time Iser hurled a knife, her whole body would convulse. With folks focused on her torment, Iser couldn't show off his talent. More to the point, the act was propagandistically ambiguous: Soldiers were made to feel sympathy for the enemy, while officers wondered why Iser, dressed like them, wasn't able to slaughter his victim.

So the shtick was nixed. Iser added daggers to his juggling gig. And Heyh? Useless for performance, she was left to clean up after the troupe.

Every night, they played for a different audience, always to a packed house. While they didn't earn the money they had in their own country, they were as popular as entertainers can be only in a state of war. Eventually, after several weeks of success, they got an invitation to play for the monarch.

Of course, His mute Majesty hadn't made the overture. The idea had come from one of his most senior advisers, formerly courtier to the king's father, who recalled that the future sovereign had been amused by acrobatics as an infant. Medically speaking, that kind of psychological twaddle lacked the reputation of a good leeching, but no authority is as strong as desperation, and, if the fighting went on much longer, there'd be no country for the ailing king to cure. A tent was propped. Ropes were tied. Shimmel rode in, standing on a horse. The show began.

The performance was spectacular that afternoon. Since the king stood on the side of neither army, commanding everybody and nobody, the troupe performed in sleek red costumes formerly used as undergarments by the disbanded palace guard. Iser juggled fire on the trapeze while Hinde and Hodel performed gymnastic somersaults on the high wire. Even the most dour advisers were enraptured, standing on their feet to see Koppel lie down on his bed of flame, and Fishke vanish him in a quilt of fire. Who could be bothered to look after the king, slumped on his throne, hands held over his ears, eyes shut, head dropped? Who was there to notice his despair?

He'd been a handsome man before the war, a natural athlete who wore his crown as lightly as a hero's laurels. Most folks had assumed that he ruled with equivalent ease, as if an unerring instinct for justice were the fulcrum of his balance, the origin of his poise. Having never seen him in his private rooms, brooding on the effects of his decisions, his subjects couldn't have fathomed what their confidence cost him in doubt. He'd taken all the blame, as if the world were his consequence. After the quake, shaken silent, he'd set aside all the old regalia. The throne he preferred was a wooden chair. His advisers, wary of adverse publicity, kept him close and enjoyed his luxuries on his behalf: the rich foods, the fancy dress, and, on this particular afternoon, the circus.

Teyvel swallowed his last sword. Schprintze disentangled herself from Hodel and Hinde, who were holding her while she juggled with Iser. Shimmel took a final gallop around the ring, bringing the show to a rousing close. A standing ovation. A royal reception. All the king's men joined the troupe in a toast. As the liquor flowed, the festivities spilled out of the tent.

Quietly, Heyh emerged from a box in the corner, dragging a tattered broom behind her. She wore pieces of the different uniforms, given to her when she still had a place on the stage as Iser's human target, a pied patchwork salvaged from the last scraps of her ruptured career. She started to sweep up horse manure—and slipped in it. As she righted herself, she thought she heard a familiar sound. A laugh.

She looked up. The room was empty, except for a man in a wooden chair, regarding her in a way she'd never seen before, laughing, yet, it seemed, not quite at her. She tested this strange idea by pretending to check whether the floor was sturdy, and then, too confidently stepping forward, feigning falling through. The man laughed again, a little louder. Then she saw what was unusual about him, for it had stretched out into the fullness of his face. Even through her blurry blue eyes, she could see that he was not sneering, but smiling.

As she got up, she smiled back at him. He clapped. She curt-sied, and, gathering a couple of Teyvel's swords, began to juggle them. They got ahead of her. She shuffled forward to catch up. They got more out of hand. Her shuffle burst into a march. Then, in an exaggerated military step—a circular advance for an army of one—she double-timed. Faster and faster, she chased her own behind. All the swords got away. She gasped and covered her head as the sharp blades stabbed into hard dirt. Rather than curtsy when the man laughed, she gave a salute.

On horseback and tightrope, she recalled more that she'd

seen of the war. She mimicked it, inexplicable to her, until the man watching her was wallowing in mirth.

She climbed onto the trapeze, high above. Seating herself on the beam, she dropped into a slouch. She covered her ears, shut her eyes, and set her face in a pout. The laughter ceased. She raised her head, and lost her balance. She fell off.

And into the man's arms. He knelt, setting her on her feet. His first words were, *Will you marry me?*

Heyh had never been asked a question like that. In fact, she'd never been asked anything, except as the rhetorical punch line to a round of abuse, so she didn't know what to respond. She tried the only reply that came into her head: *Yes.*

The man kissed her. All at once, she knew that she'd given the right answer, the only possible one, as fixed in eternity as the stars in the sky. She grabbed his sleek hair, to kiss him again.

He brought her outside, holding her large hand inside his own. He brought her to the middle of the festivities, and, standing on a barrel of ale, announced their betrothal. Bewildering as it was for his advisers to hear His Majesty speak after nearly three years, they were even more flabbergasted by what he was telling them.

— You can't marry her. She's a . . .

Heyh spoke with confidence, facing the crowd.

— I am a clown.

— A clown can't marry a . . .

Heyh turned to her betrothed

— Sir, who *are* you?

— I am the king.

— And you want to marry me anyway?

— If you'll marry a buffoon.

The king ordered his subjects to stop fighting. He spoke clearly, enunciating every word, but in the din of war, he wasn't heard. He raised his voice. He spoke from the balcony of his palace in the east, and his castle in the west: *The war is absurd,* he said.

Nobody laughed. If folks got the joke, they didn't show it.

The king had notices posted in every town, revoking all military commissions and forbidding soldiers from obeying generals' orders. The threat of peace intensified fighting. The leaders of each army made their troops believe that His Majesty was ridiculing their hard-fought suffering. The king's advisers fled the country—afraid to be associated with a man who seemingly had betrayed everybody—smuggled out by the circus in jester outfits: Shimmel and company had endured enough violence already.

The monarch was left alone with his betrothed. They'd nobody to marry them, so they simply behaved as if the deed were done. Hidden in barns and shacks, they made a palace of their embrace. They healed each other. They healed together.

But this was not a time to live happily ever after. A farmer heard their lovemaking and turned in the king to the local militia for—had he fallen so low?—half a sack of potatoes. Heyh escaped only because nobody believed she could be queen. Folks sneered, and left her behind.

She went looking for him. She stumbled through the night, nearsighted, directionless. She walked into the dawn. The sun swelled over the earth's cusp. Then she realized where she was: What she'd mistaken for the end of the world was the rift between east and west.

Heyh was no longer lost. She saw what had to be done. The king would die unless his land was healed. She scampered past the front line, where folks were just waking up. While the sentries tried to figure out what side she was on in her motley uniform, she reached the fault line, and fell inside.

Standing up, she found that the rift was just about as deep

as she was tall. Not as bad as she'd thought. With her large hands, she dug in, and started pulling at the land.

For several minutes, the soldiers on both sides watched her, holding fire as she tried to work the land loose, and draw it close. The soldiers watched and watched until one of them, a sixty-year-old infantryman, started to snicker.

— What's so funny?

— She thinks she can fix the country by might.

— Ridiculous.

— And here we are, working three years to break it by force.

— So you're laughing at her?

— I'm laughing at us.

His comrades got it, then. They chuckled along with him. Soon it was the whole battalion, enough so that Heyh could hear them. She hesitated. She listened, for she'd developed a good ear, and heard that it wasn't a jeer. The sound was warmer, not hitting her, but embracing her like the king, her lover. She recalled what she'd done for him the day they met. She exaggerated her efforts, amplified her expressions. If she couldn't move the land, at least she could move its inhabitants.

Laughter spread over the battlefield, ripples cresting into waves. Soldiers dropped their weapons, and generals their ambitions, joining their voices in the mass hysteria, carrying it clear across the countryside. They made such a ruckus that the ground began to rumble. The whole land shook. The earth quaked. And the rift closed.

Folks on both sides surged forward. They crossed the fault line. They'd scarcely have noticed it, so embattled was the surrounding terrain, were they not looking, and asking one another: What happened to the clown?

Heyh was gone. Pulled from the wreckage of his dungeon, the king was brought to where people remembered seeing her before the ground closed. *There was a clown here,* they said. She was lost when the land came together.

At first they thought he was laughing. Then they saw the tears, and knew that she'd been something to him, maybe everything, and their wonderment opened into mourning.

The kingdom turned to tears that evening, on every laughing face. The earth was bathed in their salt water, and healed together as the flooding dried.

VOV THE WHORE

There once was a region where folks cultivated secrets like turnips. The land was so poor that to grow anything at all took generations of expertise about seasons and seeds. In good years, people had food to share, a harvest feast that lasted a week, culminating in a garland of weddings. But in drought, farmers kept to their own soil, raising crops using routines and rituals guarded more jealously than wife and family.

The rain hadn't come in ages when Vov's mother married her to Ezra the widower. The girl was sixteen. The last harvest had been when she was twelve, and five suitors had proposed to her. Her father, however, had decreed that she wasn't ready for matrimony, especially to the one she loved.

— How would you know, Vov?

— Ben brings me daffodils.

— And I bring food to the table. Shouldn't *I* have your affections?

Her father had then taken what was meant for a husband, and Ben had married Vov's cousin. That winter, the clouds had gone dry, Vov's father had died, and the girl had lost her mind.

At least that's what folks said, seeing her wander through

the woods, murmuring harvest songs to herself, searching for daffodils. She missed meals, and declined to bathe or wear clothes. Neglect accentuated her beauty, sculpting her small body, stripping it down like a river eroding stone. Every day, men gazed at young Vov passing in the distance, a short stretch of white flesh in an ankle-length wrap of black hair, and comforted themselves that their wives, though homelier, had more sense than she.

Ezra, however, had last been widowed before Vov was born. He was a big man emptied by age, who'd lost not one but three wives, young women wed and gone without bringing him a child in compensation. Someone who buries spouses so regularly may get pity, but he isn't likely to be offered folks' daughters too frequently. So old Ezra had married Vov as eagerly as her mother had dispensed with her. He'd accepted a dozen eggs as dowry, yet her real value to him, since he'd sent his mule to slaughter, was to pull his plow—a labor to which he accustomed her in lieu of a honeymoon.

There were many secrets to this practice. In the first place, Ezra plowed only at night, to free the sunlight from his soil. Furthermore, rather than driving straight lines, he made his furrows labyrinthine, so intricate that not a drop of water could escape his acre plot. And then, since he lacked sufficient excrement, he fertilized the ground by uttering dirty words wherever he went.

Vov had learned these words from her father in a different context, of which she was reminded when Ezra said them, and, though they clogged her bowels with dread, they also left an expectant tingling, like a supper bell chiming, in the cleft between her legs. Her husband's cussing, however, never led there; the closest he came to touching her was with a whip over the shoulders.

Then one day the plow's blade broke. In a good year, that would have been easy to repair: Ben had a farm down the road, and in his barn he kept a grindstone. Ever since the rain had gone, though, Ezra and Ben had scarcely spoken, lest either inadvertently let the other in on a secret, and lose his singular strategic edge on fate. Ezra worried that even asking to borrow the grindstone would betray some life-and-death information, that his phrasing might convey the rhythm of his crop rotation, or that his choice of words, by painstaking recombination, might reveal to Ben some sacred truth about his farm unknown even to him. Obviously, he couldn't take that sort of risk. He could not personally make his request. So he sent his wife, whose empty-headed simplicity perfectly suited her to the task.

Vov had not spoken to Ben since her father had disengaged them four years before. In that time, he'd grown. He had the full black beard worn by all men in the region, shoulders the envy of oxen, and hands as broad as shovels, which he set on his hips as he saw Vov pulling a cart across the meadow.

— This is no place to look for daffodils, little girl.

— I don't need flowers anymore. I have a husband.

— And why has the old widower sent you here? What does Ezra want?

— He wants to borrow your grindstone.

— Why should I lend it? Did he send you to bait me? You may still be pretty, but everyone knows you lost your mind after you turned me down. Ezra wants to use my grindstone, does he? Little fool, come with me.

He led Vov to a windowless shed, barred the door behind her. His grip firmed on her shoulders. He spun her around, ripping away her dress, and thrust her back onto a damp slab.

— When you were twelve, you left me half-cocked in a field. This time, you aren't leaving so easily. And you'd best not tell, little wench. You know how to keep a secret?

Vov tried to speak. He shoved a fist into her mouth and, a

moment later, another into her cleft. Except the second fist wasn't one because he still had a hand on her neck, and then she felt a jabbing between her legs like the battering with which her father had often met her in darkness, only much, much stronger. Ben cussed and spat. He knocked her over. Her head smacked rock. Her mind went blank.

Vov awoke alone. Her body was spread on the ground, bisected by a blade of light shining through the open door of Ben's shed. She saw that her sex was violet like a bruise, and found that her head, crusted with blood, had hit Ben's grindstone.

Standing pained her, yet not in the vague way that she hurt from Ezra's incessant whipping. There was a sharpness to her condition, a quickening in her thinking, a welling of awareness that had eluded her ever since her father had broken into her and forced her mind to hide. She took a breath. Cloistering Ben's secret between her legs, she pulled on her dress, loaded her cart with the grindstone, and hauled the rock home.

After a day of honing, Ezra ran out of oil. He ordered his wife to barter some for him. He brought her a jar of pickled tomatoes from the cellar, and sent her several miles to see Meir the lender.

Vov hadn't eaten tomatoes in ages—she wasn't sure how long, since nobody had taught her to count—but she guessed it had been at least as many years as there were fruits in the jar. She sat down at the roadside and ate one. Some birds landed at her feet, ravens who mistook her, by the black of her hair, for a relative. They pecked at the seeds that spilled between her toes. She shared. They feasted. When the jar was empty, she sang them a harvest song. They alighted, all calling her name.

Hearing the squalling above, taking it for a swelling storm, Meir gathered his amply larded gut and plodded outside on gout-bloated feet. He raised a cascade of chins to the sky, squinting into the sun as the last ravens scattered. He looked out onto his fields. He leered as Vov strolled toward his house.

She nodded at the lender. She said that her husband had sent her to fetch some whetstone oil. He stopped staring. His face creased into a frown.

— Ezra knows that I don't work on credit when there's a drought. What will he trade for it?

— He was going to barter some pickled tomatoes.

— Give them to me. We'll see if they're tasty.

— They're very tasty. I ate them already.

— You're as dotty as folks say. If you took them for yourself, little pretty, then what do you have for me?

— Something more to your taste, maybe?

— And what's that?

— It's a secret.

To show the lender what she meant, she lifted her dress.

Meir was expert at judging meat on the hoof. He tweaked her breast, slapped her ass. He grunted and then, turning her around, knelt her over his doorstep. He opened his britches, grasped her shoulders, and shoved his girth against her rear. Once, twice, three times, his waves of fat washed over her back, and then she felt a slight tickle at her crotch, a trickle of warmth.

He released her. She turned over to request the oil once more. He nodded. *A deal is a deal,* he grumbled, bringing her a small canister, *even with a whore.*

On her way home, Vov began to ponder. She thought in terms that would never have occurred to her the previous day, let alone in years before. If Ben's battering had made Vov perceive her body again, negotiation with Meir proved that it wasn't all of her. A whore's possession, her flesh, could be bartered. Perhaps she could even use it for her own pleasure?

To test this idea, she detoured off the road and knocked at handsome Chaim's door.

Like every man, Chaim had watched Vov over the years—he was another of those who'd proposed when she was twelve—and he marveled at how the seasons since then hadn't changed her: While his wife, Esther, was also sixteen, beneath the warp of age and stretch of children, he could barely see the pretty girl he'd once married. Yet on Vov, dumb to time, the years had no traction. Seasons took their measure only in the spectacular span of her hair.

— It's grown so long.

— Do you like it, Chaim?

— What are you implying?

In an instant, she'd untied it. It cascaded over her shoulders. She invited Chaim under.

He was twice her height. He lifted her until their mouths met, and, as he let her down, held on to her dress. She smiled. Grasping his neck, she straddled his hips and fed him her breasts.

Chaim didn't need to tell her that what happened next was a secret, but he said so anyway.

— Esther wouldn't understand.

— You mean you don't have secrets with her?

— She's my wife. Most of our secrets are together.

— She's lucky. Would you like to share another?

That night, Vov tried to share a secret with her husband. In the dark, she went naked to his bed. Slipping in, she sought his mouth with her lips, and slid a hand up his crotch. Nothing stirred. She wondered if he'd expired, but could hear him still wheezing. For a while she listened. Only in her sleep could she hear that he was weeping.

In the morning, he was rougher with her than he'd ever

been before. He strapped her in the plow and hurled verbal filth at her. She smiled expectantly. He tore her dress from her shoulders. She shrieked delightedly. He grabbed a whip. She raised her rump to take his secret. She shut her eyes.

And felt nothing.

She looked between her knees. Saw Ezra convulsing at her feet. Was he in ecstasy without her? Vov waited until he'd stopped shuddering. She slipped out of the yoke. His body was slack.

So he was dead like her father. Vov knew that cadavers were put underground because it was dark there, a perpetual midnight, which naturally made eternal sleep easier for the deceased. She grabbed her husband's feet. She dragged him through the dirt. She put him in the cellar, under a shelf of preserved fruit.

After that, she was more free. She visited several farms each day. The men grew accustomed to seeing her, keeping their secrets with her, renewed on hayloft or under dormer. If she was hungry, she made them ply her with dainties from their cellars, for which she'd negotiate, on most favorable terms, when they were least able to resist her. If she was horny, she made them fold and bend her according to her pleasure, driving them past exhaustion with allusions to more virile partners. She did not try to hide the blemishes left by others, the gradual ravaging of her body now that time had grasp of her—now that she was alive—and if men asked about old Ezra, whether he was blind to her secret affairs, she'd say that nothing roused him anymore.

Vov the whore had more lovers each week. Gluttonously, she accumulated more secrets. But gradually she suspected that, while the secrets were new, they weren't especially different: She began to sense that truly everyone had the same secret, only a unique way of expressing it. For all their posturing, folks had nothing to hide.

Certainly she couldn't disguise that she was pregnant. As

her womb swelled, lovers grew wary, and refused to touch Vov, each one sure that it was his infidelity bloating her belly. Yet if men were anxious to avoid guilt by association, wives were possessed by a different inclination: The women had already reckoned that Vov had lured their husbands into adultery, and eagerly awaited a child as evidence with which to drive the harlot clear out of the country.

All of these changes were unexpected by Vov, who had so recently discovered freedom, and had no experience with consequences. With each passing day, as the child within her matured, she grew more isolated from the outside world. Like a secret, Vov was muffled in quiet. She might have suffocated had she not known that secrets were delusory, mirages spanning the distances between those who kept to themselves. Through summer and fall, she lay in bed alone, each day watching the changing seasons, while at night she dreamed of a village redeemed of secrets and their consequences. In her reveries, the redeemer was a whore.

She birthed her son in early winter. She swaddled him in her tresses of hair gone wholly silver, and nursed him on her breasts: the pink nipples that were the last tinge of her passing youth. She didn't name him, for they'd nobody to address but each other. She simply sang him harvest songs, and taught him what she knew about women and men, to prepare him for the ordeal foreseen in her sleep.

It began the following week, when Esther paid a visit, excusing her intrusion on the grounds that new mothers need the care of a neighbor. She asked Vov to let her hold the boy. One look at him, a glimpse into his cobalt eyes, told her that Chaim was the father.

— What do you call him?

— I don't. He's always with me.

— Where's Ezra? Why didn't he name the boy after his family?

— He's not here anymore.

— Then he knows the truth.

That afternoon, Esther posted a letter to the magistrate in the capital city, anonymously accusing Vov of adultery.

Several days later, Ben's wife, Rachel, came to the farm, claiming she'd brought the baby a gift. While Vov unfolded a tattered blanket, Rachel looked over the child, and determined, by studying his oblong ears, that Ben had fathered him.

— Was Ezra surprised to have a son after so many years?

— He didn't. The child's my own.

The encounters came more regularly after that. Vov was visited by the wife of every man she'd ever known. And every woman found that the boy, by the curve of his nose or the jut of his chin or the splay of his toes, unequivocally resembled her husband.

Vov calmly observed each moment of recognition, just as she had dreamed. The magistrate in the capital city, on the contrary, could not comprehend the sudden influx of letters about her, sometimes two or three a day, anonymously accusing her of adultery.

In and of themselves, missives such as these were not rare: Wives sent them, unsigned, all the time, and the magistrate would respond by dispatching his bailiff to extract a confession from the errant woman. For the sake of consistency, a guilty plea was required. The mandatory punishment was exile for life.

But the present case was different. If the accused had simultaneously birthed a son with each of these women's husbands, then she was a demon and couldn't be punished. On the other hand, if she wasn't a demon, and her children weren't legion, then something terrible must have possessed the whole village. For the first time in decades, the magistrate left the capital city to investigate.

His bailiff rode ahead of him, reaching the region before dawn, rousing each family, herding them to Ezra's parched farm. Men, women, children: Folks who hadn't seen one another in years, ever since the last great harvest, were brought together. They huddled for warmth, but, curiosity smothered in secrecy, didn't speak to one another.

At last, the magistrate arrived in his royally appointed carriage, painted scarlet and gold to match the colors of his velvet cloak. A footman laid down a platform for him, on which he stood, twisting the white threads of his beard, while the bailiff ousted Vov from her bed. He harried her into her clothes, and led her, child in arms, to the inquisition. The magistrate held up his staff and commanded her to confess.

— You shall not lie. You will tell the kingdom what you have done.

— I have given birth. To a son.

— Where is your husband?

— I don't have one.

— You were married to Ezra the widower.

— He died two summers ago.

— Then he isn't the father. You admit that there's no chance.

— See for yourself. You'll find Ezra in the cellar.

While the bailiff went to verify her claim, the magistrate turned to the assembled villagers.

— The accused has confessed to having a child out of wedlock. Who is the father?

Nobody spoke, not even a murmur. The magistrate shook his head. He bade his footman to bring him his docket, from which he withdrew a letter and read the first anonymous accusation of adultery he'd received.

Vov didn't object to what was written. Everyone else feigned astonishment. The magistrate waited impatiently until they stopped. Then he read another letter, and a third, letting them fall to the breeze as Vov readily agreed with each. He counted off dozens more—twenty-four more irate wives, twenty-four more seduced husbands, twenty-four more illegitimate children—and released them to the wind. Nobody moved as the paper swept through the crowd. At last the bailiff returned from his errand. He confirmed that Ezra was dead.

— Then who is the father, Vov? You acknowledge every anonymous accusation, as many letters as there are families in your village, yet you have only one son.

— But don't you see? I shared my body as a secret with every man. I took some of each inside of me. Now some of every man is in my son. All of them share him as a secret. All are his father.

— That's abnormal, Vov. It's abominable.

— The secrecy?

— The biology. Hand over the boy. I'm taking him with me.

— He's my child.

— You're bound for exile, trollop. He'll go to the university, where they'll slice him open to find out how this happened.

The magistrate began to walk toward Vov. Chaim stepped in front of him, and told the magistrate not to touch his son. The bailiff dragged him into the dust. Ben took his place, and repeated what Chaim had said. The bailiff removed him from the magistrate's path. Meir blocked the way with his great girth. The bailiff shoved him into the dirt. Each husband in the village successively stepped up, and was ousted.

As the women watched, they started asking questions: If every man had the same secret, and every woman knew it, who was deluded? None could say, nor could they be sure what else was common knowledge. Talking up seasons of sown silence, sharing the routines and rituals they'd each so assiduously hoarded, the women discovered that all their secrets, so carefully cultivated, were as similar as turnips.

By then the bailiff had cleared the last man, and had seized hold of Vov, while the magistrate, beard trembling, wrenched the baby from her hands. The child cried out. His wailing thundered across the sky, tears pouring down.

At once all the fathers rose, bolstered by their wives. Together they were much stronger. They hauled away the bailiff and ousted the magistrate. They eased the sobbing child to his mother's breast. As the boy began to nurse, the tempest lifted. Folks looked up, into falling rain. Mother and child stood by their new family, cleansed by the roiling storm.

ZAYIN THE PROFANE

Zayin never asked to be the Messiah. Daughter of the village apothecary, a widower named Menashe, she already had plenty of responsibility for a thirteen-year-old girl. For example, she had to wake up every morning at dawn, to dust and sweep her father's little shop. And in the afternoon, while he napped upstairs, she had to stand on tiptoe at the counter, taking orders.

Zayin was a good girl. She didn't complain, even when her father sent her to houses where boys tormented her with unsolicited kisses, and taunted her for spurning their advances with accusations that she and her papa were too affectionate. She didn't understand, quite, what they meant, but she knew that she loved him alone in the world, and would do anything at all for his sake, as he'd done everything for her. She intended to be his helpmeet forever, as young girls will, and her efforts played no small part in the prosperity of his shop: His prescriptions were as effective as could be expected, never deadly, yet it was her light step as she delivered those medications, her still voice and gentle smile, that nursed folks most. Nobody liked to pass a whole winter without a head cold. And, in summer, when she wore flowers in her hair, there was a veritable epidemic of hay fever. Illness lost its stigma in the village on account of young Zayin. People even looked forward to new ailments, as a gourmand longs for the pangs of hunger.

How else to explain the town's attitude toward rumors of a great plague sweeping the countryside? At first the news came from shiftless old cadgers, flea-bitten beggars peddling rat-eaten clothes swindled from the dead. They swore that they'd seen whole cities extinguished in a breath, and had endured the crush, escaped the holocaust, only because death prefers to embrace fresh youth. Ordinarily, local rowdies would have ousted those filthy old men with sticks and stones, and the village aldermen would have taken the additional precaution of barring the town's gates, but the reputation of Menashe the apothecary made folks confident that there was nothing to worry about—and perhaps a visit from Zayin to anticipate. Even the initial influx of refugee families from the east the following day merely made villagers wonder why every town couldn't have a good druggist with a pretty daughter to assuage their cares.

Only Menashe was distraught. He cautioned that his medicines could not cure a plague, but folks were too keenly occupied, watching refugees arrive and die, to hear what he had to say. And then it was too late.

An eighteen-year-old peasant named Fayvel was the first villager to complain. He claimed that a devil sat on his chest while he slept, stealing his breath. His brothers wanted to know what the dybbuk looked like, but he didn't know because the creature vanished the moment he awoke. After a few days, the demon came up with a cleverer idea: Instead of floating off at dawn—devils naturally lose their mortal weight in daylight—the beast climbed down inside Fayvel's lungs. There it was always dark; the night never ended, and Fayvel, become but a second skin for the demon, always slept.

Unable to rouse him with pinpricks or lamp burns, his

brothers visited the apothecary. Menashe's shop was already crowded with relatives of folks who, while not yet as ill as poor Fayvel, already couldn't breathe in their sleep. They begged the druggist for an elixir that would lift this evil. They reached out hands heavy with silver, but he simply stood behind his counter, arms in the air, hollering over the din that, medically speaking, there was nothing to be done.

Upstairs, Zayin listened to the commotion. She'd never heard such noise in the shop, but strangest to her of all sounds was the voice of her own father: In her thirteen years, she hadn't once heard him shout, or turn someone down.

After several hours, Menashe cleared out his shop. He came up to take a nap. Zayin wished to ask him many questions, but her fear that he'd yell at her, as he'd shouted at his patients, made her quiet. She kept out of his way. From the corner, she watched him haul his body into bed. He called her over. Shutting his eyes, he murmured that she didn't need to tend the shop, as he'd already locked it up. Then he folded his hands over his belly, and fell into a heavy sleep.

After a while, Zayin grew tired of being idle. Intending to sweep the floors, she wandered downstairs, where she saw some men at the door. She let them in. Fayvel's three brothers crowded around her, all at once trying to explain what was the matter.

— Fayvel will die if the devil inside him isn't doused.

— I'm sure my father can fix a tonic. I'll bring it tonight.

— There's no money for anything fancy.

— I'll tell Papa not to make you pay. He'll understand. He's good that way.

She sent them home and started to clean, pleased to be doing more than was expected of her. She dusted the sills, and was about to polish the countertop when her father came to her.

— Were those men's voices I heard?

— Fayvel's brothers were here. He needs a tonic to get the devil out of him.

— It isn't a dybbuk, Zayin. It's a plague.

— Whatever it is, Fayvel needs some medicine. I promised to bring a draft to him tonight.

— You don't understand. I closed the shop for a reason. I haven't got a remedy for Fayvel. I can't make one.

— Because of his money?

— Stupid girl! Listen to me. A plague is deadly. I have a cure for nobody.

— Papa, you can do anything. You're an apothecary. Why are you yelling at me?

He shook his head and led her up a ladder to the attic laboratory.

She had never been there before, amid his bottled secrets, shelved alphabetically according to arcane names pronounced by no one since the fall from Eden. Ancient roots and pollens smuggled from that model garden into the mortal world: Like every apothecary, Zayin's father trafficked in sacred contraband, distillations of eternity that, administered in the right combination and quantity, were said to lend a body grace with which to clear the evils of disease, but that, drunken gratuitously, might disburden soul of flesh. Menashe watched his daughter peer into his stone crucible, tap on the copper basin of his still, lift the heavy bronze pestle from its mortar, and set it down again. When at last she'd satisfied her curiosity, and could appreciate what he did, he told her that nothing she saw there, neither equipment nor stock, made the least medicinal difference.

Naturally, the girl was perplexed. Was this not his only laboratory? Was there another ladder yet to climb? Were there attics and ladders stacked, invisible except from within, all the way to the heavens? She wondered if her father might be more than just a druggist, but before she could inquire, Menashe had uncorked one of the priceless powdered mysteries on his shelf, and held it out to her: *Confectioners' sugar,* he said, and, when she didn't believe him, he had her taste for herself. With the utmost care, she pointed a slender finger into the powder, and touched it to her tongue. The uncut sweetness burned.

Before she could pose a question, he let his daughter know the whole formula. He said that the antidote to an illness wasn't the product of a laboratory, nor did it grow in a garden. It came from within the patient. The active ingredient, so to speak, was hope. If folks believed that his pills and tonics worked miracles, they sometimes indirectly did—more often than the harsh chemicals with which city doctors routinely massacred the sick. The city doctors claimed to practice science, but Menashe had studied enough to know what they didn't, and to acknowledge what they wouldn't. He said that, given a chance, the body was a finer apothecary than the most learned chemist, but that people placed their faith elsewhere, in elixirs. His nontoxic pills and tonics simply concentrated folks' faith, the belief that they were entitled to another draft of life, and directed it back inside, where it belonged.

Zayin took in her father's words, and knew that he was wise. Only one matter confused her.

— If it's that simple, why can't I just bring Fayvel a tincture of sugar water? If he thinks that it's a remedy . . .

— The body is a good apothecary, Zayin, but a plague cannot be cured. Fayvel won't survive. Everyone who catches it will die. If I waste my reputation on hopeless cases, my medicines won't be as potent against lesser disease. Be practical, and don't go outside, or let anyone in. The plague will pass in a few weeks, but for now there's no knowing who's sick.

Fayvel's brothers were preparing for another all-night vigil, loading the hearth with coal, when the apothecary's daughter arrived at their hovel. In her hushed voice, she asked if the patient was still alive. They pointed to his bed by the fire. She smiled. She asked to be left alone with him, and, because the estimable Menashe was her father, they went off to sleep in the hayloft.

The girl was gone before dawn. Fayvel's brothers didn't see her leave. They gathered around him. One of them leaned on his chest, to feel if he was breathing. He gasped. Sighed. He opened his eyes. He asked for Zayin. They didn't know what to tell him.

— I asked her to marry me. She wouldn't do it.

— Because you're dying, Fayvel.

— Not anymore. Do I seem sick still?

While Fayvel hardly looked prepared to plow a field, his brothers had to admit that even his ability to talk bespoke progress. They wanted to know which of Menashe's drugs the girl had given him. He swore that she'd brought none, yet he couldn't say what she'd done to bring about his unexpected recovery. He could recollect only that she'd been clutching his hands for a long time and talking to him, whispering, really, when the demon in his chest released him, or, perhaps, he released the demon.

— What was she saying? Was she praying? Did she cast a spell?

— I don't know what she told me, but there was sense in her murmuring, and something more, a singing from elsewhere. I was scared to open my eyes, that she'd disappear forever. I held her hands tight. I looked at her. It was like staring into a sunrise. I asked her to marry me, but I knew she wouldn't. She isn't one of us.

His brothers weren't sure exactly what he meant by that. But they knew that he was right, because her voice scarcely stirred the air when she spoke and her feet barely touched the earth where she walked. She had, almost, the substance of light.

Several days passed. As Fayvel convalesced, other folks got worse. The plague threatened to suffocate whole families. Given another week, the town itself might have ceased to breathe, had Fayvel's brothers not confided to a grain merchant, whose wife lay ill, Zayin's extraordinary visitation.

— But Menashe himself pronounced that there's no earthly remedy. He's closed up shop.

— It wasn't one of his drugs that made Fayvel better. It's Zayin herself. You see, she isn't one of us.

On his way to fetch her, the grain merchant repeated what he'd heard to the miller, whose employees were too sick to work, and the miller mentioned it to the sawyer and the cooper's wife and several journeyman carpenters, and soon the whole town shared the same secret. A crowd swelled around the apothecary's door.

Menashe had spent the past couple of days securing his building against the incurable sickness and those who carried it. He'd boarded over the windows and doors of his shop with lumber, and had little Zayin climb up into the chimney flue, to pack it tight with rags. Then he'd sent her down to the basement, to see what provisions they had, and what she could make from them in days and weeks to come.

It was while she was down there that Menashe heard the clamor outdoors, louder than it had been in days, since the first tremor of the plague. For a moment he listened, but he didn't hear people shouting his name. They were calling for Zayin.

Menashe peered through the one attic window he hadn't yet boarded and sealed. He saw burghers and tradesmen and peasants, many of whom carried saws and axes in their hands. He opened the casement and leaned out over the sill.

— What do you want from me? I've told you this plague is deadly. I have no cure.

— We want your daughter.

— You want to kill her?

— We want her to save us, Menashe.

— Has the plague made you crazy? She's just a little girl.

— She revived Fayvel.

— She didn't. She couldn't.

— Zayin isn't of this world.

Menashe hurried down to the cellar. He grabbed his daughter, and demanded to know what she'd done. She told him that she'd tallied up all the carrots and beets, but not yet the onions.

— That's not what I mean. There are people outside saying that you revived Fayvel.

— Is he really feeling better?

— Is Fayvel your lover? I ordered you not to go outdoors.

— I haven't been out in days. Papa, I love only you. You taught me to care for others. How could I be true to you and let Fayvel suffer?

— You stole my medicines. You faked my prescriptions.

— I gave him no pills. I only stood by him awhile. I held his hands, in case he was in pain. I told him not to place such faith in demons. I said that I was there for him. I said that I had hope, and asked him if he'd believe in me. Then I was going to try to explain about the body being an apothecary, so he wouldn't feel bad that I hadn't brought him drugs, but he interrupted by proposing marriage to me.

— You accepted?

— Papa!

— Do you have any idea what you've done, Zayin? Can you even try to understand? Folks think you're some kind of Messiah.

The girl couldn't tell if he was proud or disgusted or simply incredulous. In silence, he led her to the attic, and pointed her to the window. More people had gathered below, and, when they saw her, their voices lifted up on her name and soared.

Zayin looked at her father, and said she had to go to them. Menashe saw that it was true. If she didn't, they'd tear the house down. He turned away, and let her leave him.

For seven days and nights, Zayin did not sleep. Straight through the sabbath she worked, tending the sick, holding their hands and murmuring her hope, insisting that they could get better, begging them to believe in her. They did, one after another. They believed that this lightning girl in long golden braids and white gossamer slip was the savior. And, one after another, they were healed by her.

Of course, religious authorities were skeptical. The head rabbi, undisputed leader of the community, several times sent his beadle to seize her, in order that there might be a proper inquisition regarding her irregular behavior, but the people wouldn't let her go. Then the old rabbi got ill. He was put to bed by his wife, a zaftig woman half his age who all but breathed for him as he lay dying. At last she called for the beadle. Leading him into a room where nobody would hear, she asked the man to tell Zayin that the rabbi needed her.

The beadle had no difficulty locating the girl: Even from the steps of the shul, he could see the crowd of tradesmen and farmers surrounding the shack where she was reviving a stricken beggar. Having one and all pledged themselves to her, they called themselves her followers—despite her efforts to send them away—and also considered themselves her protectors, earthly guardians of the miracle that had saved them and their families. They halted the beadle as he approached. He tried to explain why he'd come, how it wasn't the same as the last time, but they shouted him down.

Zayin emerged into the commotion. She asked what was wrong. The beadle held up a hand and called out to her. Fayvel and his brothers knocked him over. The mob prepared to lynch him. But as they closed in on their victim, they found that they were facing Zayin.

She was standing over the rabbi's man. She wouldn't move until the mob lost its will to be one. Then she knelt down, and let the beadle speak.

He repeated what the rabbi's wife had said to him, and implored her, on his own behalf as well, to save the holy man. She took a deep breath. She vowed to do what she could, and, against the advice of her self-appointed disciples, who predicted that it was a trap, accompanied the beadle to the rabbi's private quarters behind the shul.

Several feverish acolytes, men with eager beards, were praying there, but stopped short when they saw Zayin standing, radiant, at the door. Into the sudden silence rose the rabbi's wife, embracing the girl and saying, loud enough for all to hear, that *she* believed in her. Then she brought Zayin to the bed where the rabbi lay sleeping, and, chasing away the acolytes like vermin, left the two of them alone.

For the first time, Zayin faced the great man unseparated by the distance of ritual, the ordained space between altar and balcony. Up close he appeared more ancient than the patriarchs. Had she not seen him leading the town in worship just a few weeks before, she'd have believed that he'd been dug from the ground like an antediluvian fossil. His skin was the cast of dust, his flesh as cold as clay. She clasped his hands anyway, and, kneeling over him, laid her head on his chest.

Her words came unprepared. In her mouth, the language softened, melting into song she couldn't comprehend. The sick man began to hum. Zayin lifted her head. Her lips were no longer moving. It was always this way when her work was done: Her song was being sung by him.

The rabbi opened an eye, and regarded her.

— How do you know these words, child of Menashe?

— I don't know them, rabbi. They just come to me.

— You don't know them? They aren't known to me either, but when you chant them . . . they must be sacred.

— They come to me when I heal someone. Folks live when they accept my words as their own.

— You speak this way to a rabbi? I suppose that you have the right. But please answer me this: Why does the savior come here in the body of a girl?

— With all due respect, rabbi, I don't think I'm the savior. I'm just good at letting people get better.

— You *are* the Messiah, then. This is how you test us. You come without priestly lineage or learning, and in the flesh of the flawed sex. I'd have ordered you dead for sacrilege. You choose to revive me. What is your reason, Zayin? Won't you please tell me?

He'd closed his eyes while he spoke, to hold in the emotion. When he opened them, to look at her again, the little girl had fallen asleep, folded up at his feet.

It is said that the Messiah has been here before, more times than any mortal can imagine: Every day, the Messiah comes and goes again, and always will, until the world is fit for redemption. This phenomenon is not arcane. It has been observed by everyone who has witnessed a sunrise, when the Messiah's heavenly robe drapes the earthly threshold, or seen a sunset, as the last vestiges pass, haltingly, overhead.

As Zayin's name became known across the land, people observed that the sky was different. Dusk wasn't as vivid with color as they remembered, nor was dawn as intense. A cosmic change had taken place. Folks no longer looked up for grace, but began to search in their own midst.

They were looking for a girl with golden braids and a gossamer slip. They were looking for a girl whose feet didn't touch the earth and whose voice didn't stir the air. Synagogues and yeshivas sent envoys imploring her to pass through this village or that city, for every place touched by plague suffers in myriad ways.

Zayin didn't want to go. Already she hadn't seen her father in many days, and, with the pestilence exorcised at last, she knew that he'd soon be needing her in his shop, to sweep the floors and deliver balms for ordinary aches and pains. Yet when she told the rabbi this, he demanded to know what business the Messiah had pushing a mop. He was willing to accept that the savior had breasts, but wasn't it a bit much for her to test folks' faith by keeping house for misanthropic Menashe while the whole world struggled? Uncertain as she was that she was who he believed her to be, she had to admit that, on the chance that he was right, she was wrong to behave so selfishly. Late at night, while her disciples slept, she left.

In the first village she reached, everyone was mourning the dead. That's all they did, day and night, since the plague had churlishly taken away parents and children and sisters and brothers and wives and husbands and lovers and friends, leaving the lives of those who remained desperately incomplete.

Rain was falling when Zayin arrived, so much that the streets were flooded, yet, as soon as she spoke, scores of people came outside, arms outstretched, to greet her through their tears: While ceaseless hours of saline sorrow had washed away their vision—a mercy for those who no longer had family to see—her unwavering voice told them that the Messiah was in their midst, to answer their prayers by ending their anguish. They wanted to bring her into the great hall, where they'd prepared a banquet with the last of their harvest, but she declined. For a while she stood, silent and still, in the town square. Rain flowed through her cotton frock, and down her pale skin, as she waited until everyone was quiet, and a voice came to her.

She asked if folks didn't notice the water pouring down

from the sky. They did, and again urged her to come inside. She shook her head, and then, because they were blind, she said:

— Don't you people know what it is, this storm above, and why it won't end? Don't you recognize the cry of your dead?

— What have they got to be upset about?

— They're mourning.

— Mourning who?

— Mourning all of you.

— We're still alive.

— You don't look it, from their point of view. You don't farm. You don't trade. Today is one of your festivals but you don't dance or feast. The dead are gone, and cannot return. How can they know if you live, that all is not lost, when you pass your lives in secret? If you want this downpour to stop, be done with your own tears first.

She led them to their great hall. The banquet began. Hesitantly at first, folks drank and ate. Timidly at first, they sang and danced. Gradually their revelry filled the night, poured over into the new day. In sunlight, they found that they could see again. They saw that there was no more rain. They looked for Zayin, savior of the living and dead. They searched everywhere for a girl with golden hair, but their Messiah, good work done, was gone.

She arrived that day in a city where everyone constantly fought. They'd been warring ever since the plague had decimated their population, taking away the powerful and rich, leaving a wealth of opportunity for those who endured, and, with it, an epidemic of greed.

Folks didn't pick up on Zayin right away—incessant bickering had deafened them—but from the moment that she was noticed, every man and woman demanded a private appointment. Each claimed personally to have invited her to the city, in order that she might resolve their conflict before the shouting crumbled buildings. Beholden to her faithful as a king is to his subjects, she did as she was bidden. She met with each person alone, and by everyone was told why opportunity couldn't be shared by the many, and what uniquely gave him or her—and not another soul—exclusive claim to the chance at hand. She listened with sympathy, and was unsettled to find that everyone was in agreement. Were the men and women correct, one and all, that chance didn't divide evenly, and opportunity, unless exploited individually, was just an empty promise? Wise Menashe would have known the answer, but of course Zayin couldn't rely on her father anymore: A Messiah is sui generis. She straightened her shoulders, took a breath, and, as ever, let the words swell within her. *You're right,* she told each claimant, slowly so her lips could be read, *but the opportunity is not yours to take.*

— Whose is it, then?

— You must listen: It belongs to the first person whose words you hear.

Folks shut their mouths after that. They cleaned their ears. There were advantages to be had simply by knowing who'd been chosen, opportunity within occasion, like the seeds inside an orange. And so it came to pass, after many months of quiet calm, that people heard again.

Yet it didn't happen all at once, to the sound of a single voice. On the contrary, each person heard opportunity in somebody different: Everyone was chosen by someone. Epidemic greed gave way to contagious cooperation. They rebuilt the city. They built to honor Zayin.

By then, she was long gone. She had been to a hundred cities and towns. Folks reported miracles wherever her gaze fell. Her voice made plague-ruined villages flourish. Old ghosts were vanquished. Mothers had new children.

People sought to worship Zayin, and she permitted it, as long as it was done by grazing livestock or tilling the soil. Some grumbled that such profane activities had nothing to do with her eternal glory. Patiently, she reminded them that the world was the Messiah's twin, born of the same creation, and to treat either well was to honor the other. They did what she asked. They tended the earth, and, when they prospered, they knew that Zayin had blessed them in turn.

One day, Menashe fell ill. Several years had passed since he'd last seen Zayin, and the burden of running his shop had become wholly his own. They'd not been easy years. Folks had forgiven his churlishness during the pestilence only because the Messiah was—at least according to birth records—his own daughter. Even so, he sold far fewer elixirs than before. For the state of his business, he'd a bitter diagnosis, from which he drew a sort of long-suffering comfort: Zayin's little savior shtick had cured the land of hypochondria, patron ailment of his trade, by drugging people silly with hope. Abandoned by his prodigal daughter, unable to afford help, he had to go out, an old man, in the chill of winter, peddling balms no one wanted anymore. He caught cold. He took to bed. He would have no medicine. Drugs were as false to him as Zayin.

On the third day of Menashe's illness, the old rabbi came to his house. The apothecary was sleeping, and couldn't be roused. The rabbi tried to recollect the benediction that Zayin had given when he'd been sick, words as certain yet unfamiliar to him as his own birth. How could a scholar who was able to recite the entire Kabbalah not retain those few simple sounds? And why did the effort to remember them make him forget, for a trembling moment, even how to breathe? If he kept up the attempt, he knew he'd be lost to it. Forgetting birth is the price of life; were it not forgotten, nothing else would make an impression.

He surrendered. Instead of playing prophet, he wrote a letter imploring Zayin, wherever in the world she was, to come home before her father—the one who had raised her—was dead and gone. He copied his missive ten times, and sent it to ten other rabbis. He requested that each do the same. Then he returned to Menashe, and waited while his words radiated across the continent.

There wasn't yet any snow on the ground that winter, but, within days, the countryside was white with paper. Whole forests fell as letters begat letters, cascading from town to town, touching down in urgent flurries, rising up in a storm front.

Zayin had been in the same village for several days, the longest she'd spent in one place since she began her sojourn. The town wasn't especially sick or damaged, in want of complicated miracles, and she might not have spent a single night there were it not for a man she'd seen on the street and been unable to forget. He was a peddler, young yet well worn like his old copper wares, a wanderer like she'd become, except that, while she was celebrated by folks who had yet to meet her, he was anonymous even among people to whom he was familiar.

Zayin could not stop looking at him. She wondered if she'd met him before, if she'd saved him and was drawn to him protectively, as mother to son. She wondered if she was somehow related to him, if they shared the same blood, a continent apart, as distant cousins. She wondered a hundred wonders, but nothing she had known, or even imagined, could explain the intensity of his presence, his absolute singularity in a marketplace crowded with men and donkeys: A glimpse of him made her lose sight of all humanity. In his dawn-blue eyes, the girl Messiah perceived all that she had never thought to desire.

The first time that she saw the man, she tried to approach him, but found that many dozen of her devotees stood between them, awaiting her care. For a moment she didn't—care, that is—wouldn't have been bothered to see them slaughtered, if only they weren't in her way. She attempted to push past the hordes, yet couldn't move a limb. She looked down. She couldn't even see her legs and arms, so fiercely were folks grasping them, in want of her ministrations. Their troubles overwhelmed her. Their expectations overcame her. She yielded. Zayin was a good girl. Did it matter that she hadn't asked to be the Messiah? Her followers hadn't asked to suffer.

She returned to the marketplace the next day and the day after. Folks gathered around her with small aches and abrasions, but she couldn't find her peddler among them. She wanted to ask about him, wished she had his name. What could she say? She worked and she waited.

It was on the fourth day that news of Zayin's father at last found her, early morning in the marketplace. In the time that it took her to read the letter, ten more came, and then a hundred, a thousand. Before the blizzard of paper could smother her, the fastest horse was fetched from the mayor's stables, and saddled. A man lifted her up by the waist. In his grip, she felt a shimmer, like first light, within her. She caught his dawn-blue eyes, their blaze. His cheek brushed hers. He whispered some words in her ear. She couldn't be sure, but she thought he said, *I'm here for you, Zayin.*

Then the horse carried her across a landscape, smooth with fallen paper, to the next town, where she changed to a fresh horse, and so forth, all the way home. The rabbi received her in an embrace, and took her to Menashe. The apothecary hadn't been awake in days, the rabbi told her. He didn't drink or eat. His emaciated body rattled with death whenever he breathed.

Zayin mounted the stairs and entered his bedchamber alone. From the window, she saw that the whole town had gathered below. She turned away from them. She knelt on the floor beside Menashe's cot, and, beneath the blankets, found his hands.

The nails were already long and sharp like a cadaver's subterranean claws, yet she didn't wince, so often had she done this before, drawing men and women back into the world for another day or year. She began chanting. She put her ear to his chest to hear her words hum within him. They didn't. Instead there was a rumbling: Menashe, clearing his throat, coughing.

— Enough with the singing, Zayin.

— Hush, Papa. It's good for you. This is how I save people.

— First you run away from home and make me old because I can't rely on you. Now I'm dying and you're telling me what to do.

— You won't die.

— I'm an apothecary. I know these things.

— I'm the Messiah. Things are as I say.

— No, daughter, you're delusional. You're just an ordinary girl. I'm your father, Zayin. I'd have noticed if you had the wings of an angel. I'd have seen if you'd fallen from the heavens.

— What about my miracles?

— Don't you recall what I told you about my medicines? Do you remember how I said that they don't do anything on their own, but sometimes they work wonders just because people believe in them?

— Since the body is the best apothecary?

— Yes, Zayin. Your miracles are like my elixirs: the tricks of a charlatan.

— You're certain?

— As certain as you will be, shortly, when, in spite of your magical intervention, this sickness finally kills me. Find love, Zayin. Make a family. Life is the only miracle, and it's brief.

— At least may I sing to you?

— Sing me a lullaby, child.

As she chanted, he shut his eyes and hummed along. When she could no longer hear him, he was gone.

In the realm of human experience, only watching your parents die is more terrible than seeing your Messiah cry. After many hours, Zayin went to the window, bathed in tears, to share what had happened, and what she now knew. *My father is dead,* she exclaimed. *I am not the Messiah. Please go home.*

But how could they possibly believe Zayin? There was too much evidence against her blasphemous claims, evidence carried in their own bones: Were she not the Messiah, they wouldn't be there to be forsaken by her.

Why would she save them from the demon plague, only to abandon them? What sin had they committed to bring her to tears? What evil had they done to make her take Menashe's life and leave them? They demanded that she at least condemn them, requested the small justice of knowing the crime for which they were punished.

Zayin came down to them. Even in her anguish, she recognized that the only sin had been her messianic arrogance, and that the atonement must be her silence. She would simply let folks believe about her what they had to believe: Her crime would become her punishment.

A placebo Messiah, the apothecary's orphan wandered the land. She no longer performed miracles, nor expected them, but rather watched, breathless, as they happened, seemingly spontaneously, wherever she went. In her presence, folks found health and wealth, wisdom, even. Families ended feuds, and countries brought wars to truce. The miracles appeared more incredible than before, as if to test her, to taunt her, to torment her with the awareness she alone possessed, that she'd nothing whatsoever to do with the world in its mystery. Zayin felt like a scapegoat, except her burden wasn't blame, but credit. She had to keep moving, to escape the wrath of acclaim.

She traveled in silence for a year, and witnessed every possible astonishment, save for the one that might have moved her: the wonder of being embraced again by the man with eyes of dawn. Every day she doubted more the words she thought he'd whispered. She realized that he couldn't be there for her if she was everywhere and nowhere, a placebo human: Zayin, false Messiah, had become entirely what she was not, at the expense of who she'd once been. When miracles happened in her midst, she no longer knew who was being acclaimed. She felt neither pride nor shame. She lost all delusions, could neither see nor hear. The air gave way around her.

Zayin fainted. She'd been standing in a pasture. Folks set her on a bed of straw there. The villagers didn't know what else to do, for they'd never seen a Messiah before, much less one who was ill.

The town had neither rabbi nor shul. The mayor sent his sons to the three nearest cities. Each returned leading a veritable country. Aldermen and holy men, tradesmen and peasants: If this was the apocalypse, who didn't want to be in the midst of it? The crush to see Zayin on her cot was suffocating. She was barely breathing. She responded to nobody, nothing. Her eyes were open, unblinking. Her lips were parted, unmoving. Her skin, radiant white, began to blue.

Or so some claimed. Others insisted that the change came from up above, as the afternoon sky darkened overhead—enfolding Zayin in deepest ultramarine—and the last light vanished under a fringe of fiery red.

Zayin was swept away in the light. She cast off her body like a slip as she was carried through the night. At last she came to rest, she knew not where, only that it was not a world she had traveled before. Still she felt no fear, for she was in the grasp of something long wanting, cradling her, easing her to sleep.

Sometime later, the dawn awoke her. She looked up—into the blue eyes of her lost peddler. He wore a mantle woven of the sun's spectrum, in which he held her. She heard herself speak.

— What are *you* doing here?

— Don't you know, Zayin? I'm the Messiah.

— But you were a peddler before.

— It was something to do. The world didn't need me while you were alive.

— *I* needed you.

— You have me now.

— Will you never leave me again?

— I'll leave you every day, to cross the sky. At night, you'll be my bride.

Holding her tight, he pierced her with light. Then he left, to lead in the new morning. She watched as folks awoke and looked around, each finding that the apocalypse had not happened. One by one, they then gazed up into the dawn, and smiled. It was well that a Messiah passed above, now that Zayin, their savior, had shown them how to live.

CHET THE CHEAT

From the day that he was born, Chet was an orphan. By no means was he the only one in his town, for birth was often fatal back then, but, even by the standards of the local poorhouse, the child was pitifully thin. That may be why, on Chet's thirteenth birthday, the village sin-eater, a sallow old widower named Ephraim, picked the boy to be his apprentice.

Ephraim was the region's first sin-eating professional, a godsend, some said, for, in many rural stretches, the practice was still carried out communally: When a man or woman died, relatives would set a parting meal atop the sealed coffin, and anyone who ate a bite would consume a bit of the sin weighing down on the deceased, a portion of the wrong that the poor soul hadn't survived to metabolize. The sin would become, by common understanding, the entire family's digestive, and penitential, burden. Yet, no matter how fine the cooking—how rich the truffles or heavy the cream—folks seldom had much appetite for dead people's troubles. How much simpler folks found it, how much less expensive and more efficient, to dispense with the graveside buffet, to put out some stale bread or moldy fruit, and hire a man to eat it at night while the village slept.

Nevertheless, professional sin-eating wasn't easy. The sin-eater had to be penitent every waking hour, and had to take care never to sin, even in his dreams. While the price for Ephraim's services varied from corpse to corpse, based on his estimation of how folks lived their lives, his calculations were necessarily approximations: His rudimentary actuarial tables couldn't account for forgotten childhood slights, say, or unconfessed fratricides. The sin-eater carried in his gut the speechless guilt of all society, underbelly-by-proxy, and, if he was to avoid eternal damnation, much less sustain people's confidence in him, he had to be both more and less than human.

Ephraim accomplished that by living the life of an ascetic, and this was the basis of Chet's education. The old man had cleared a den in the side of a mountain several miles from the cemetery gates, where the boy came to live with him. Every little luxury that Chet had known—warm gruel, straw bed, sickly girls—was denied to him, and, had Ephraim not so carefully watched the boy, he might have been the first ward ever to run away *to* an orphanage.

Ephraim drilled Chet every day, to build his stamina for consuming and carrying sin, by filling his belly with sand and pebbles and rocks, and sprinting him from mountaintop to mountaintop. When he wasn't mute with agony, or bleeding too profusely, Chet questioned his master's tactics.

— Sins aren't made of stone, you know.

— That's their danger. They're much easier to swallow, Chet, and far harder to expel.

But Chet wasn't about to fall for that old-world-wisdom shtick. He taught himself to fake his swallow, and learned other tricks, too. He worked the geological gamut: With the cunning of a con artist, he chewed up granite and spat out garnets. With the bombast of a carnival showman, he made boulders vanish in a cloud of dust. Ephraim watched with horror his pupil's hunger for attention, and decided that the time had come for a new lesson.

He brought Chet to the cemetery late one night. Candles burned where meals lay in wait, table scraps slopped atop each coffin in its open crypt. There was also money, the negotiated fee, which Ephraim set aside as alms after counting it and issuing a receipt. Chet watched his master eat, the only food he'd ever seen the old man take in. Ephraim was silent, but the candle illuminating his pained face appeared to flicker, and each morsel seemed to cry in his throat. When he was done, the candle flared up, and went out.

At the final crypt, he gave the boy a crust of bread. The bread was hard, but Chet had eaten staler loaves at the orphanage. He felt none of the trembling that appeared to afflict Ephraim as it passed his gullet. He reached for more. With a broad hand, the master held him back.

— Sin is poison. You have no tolerance for it yet.

— I'll be fine. I've swallowed stones.

— You must do good before you eat again.

Ephraim made his apprentice help out the local stream, which could scarcely keep up a trickle that spring, by easing its load: For three full days, Chet hauled buckets of water to town. When he was done, Ephraim asked if he'd received gratitude from anyone.

— Folks took the water, but they laughed at me when I said that I was carrying it for the creek.

— Good. If you'd accepted praise, you'd have had to start over again.

Chet nodded, appreciating the master's point. He noted that showing off with stones and sins was not the only trick in the books, that sometimes it paid to act with discretion, leaving people to their own beliefs.

· · ·

Old Ephraim died that summer. While he had no family, everybody in town attended his funeral. Sender the rabbi declared him holy. Then food was set atop his coffin, a candle was lit, and the people left in blessed silence.

An apprentice no longer, Chet consumed the sins of his master. When he finished his meal, the candle didn't flare up—so he snuffed it with his finger. Then he fell asleep, under the weight of indigestion, beside the coffin.

Early in the morning, he was awoken by Ofer the grave digger, who wanted to know when he'd be disposing of Ephraim's corpse.

— Isn't that your job, Ofer?

— I only handle folks buried in the cemetery. Old Ephraim never bought a plot.

— The rabbi called him holy.

— It doesn't mean he had money. I don't make the rules, Chet. That's how it is for everybody. It's the way of the world.

So Chet dragged his master's putrid body—even the coffin didn't belong to him—all the way to the rabbi's study, where Sender was teaching his disciples scripture. When the students saw what was coming, they tried to deflect Chet at the door, to shove him back out into the street, without letting the putrid corpse soil their silk and sable, but Sender waved them away. Wrapping himself in a mink stole, he led Chet into the courtyard, his personal improvement on the Garden of Eden, all marble statuary and malachite cisterns. Against one of the urns, Chet rested his master's body. Then he told the rabbi how Ofer had cast beloved Ephraim out of the cemetery.

— Ephraim should have known: Credit in the world-to-come is nonnegotiable in the here-and-now.

— He had money, rabbi. He gave it away.

— He was holy. That can be impractical.

— Then what should I do with his body?

— Throw it in the forest. Leave the rest to fate.

Chet did as he was told. When he returned the next day, only bones and vultures remained.

So the sin-eater was fated to be carrion. Had Chet a mind for metaphor, he might have interpreted that in any number of ways, extracted meaning as the birds drew marrow from the bones. But Chet had no capacity for poetry. He was a practical young man, with a promising future in a respectable profession. Following the lead of the rabbi, he resolved not to be holy, but to be wealthy. He didn't want, quite, to bury himself in money as bankers did. Rather he wished to own, outright, all that the here-and-now had to offer.

That took gold, which might have been hard to obtain were Chet in any ordinary trade: Coal and grain were purchased on credit slips, but death was a one-way cash transaction. Of course, if Chet spent his sin-eating fees—if he built a mansion and bought a carriage with those coins instead of giving them away as alms—he'd have to compensate with other good deeds. He'd have to carry rivers of water to work off the sins he ingested each evening at the cemetery. For weeks he vacillated, and gave his earnings away. Then one night, while picking over the sins of a burgher's beloved wife—served up as a platter of decomposing fish—crafty Chet saw through his professional dilemma to a scheme that, he mused to himself, would have impressed even upright Ephraim.

Chet had not been back to the orphanage in the couple of years since he began his apprenticeship, but little had changed there. The widow Yidel still woke the children several hours before dawn by pounding her clogs against a tin pan. Boys were sent to chop wood in the dark forest, miles beyond the burghers' most outlandish property claims, while girls were sent to scavenge what scraps they could from the town waste bins, to scrape together a morning gruel. After that, the children were left to beg in the streets, not because anyone gave them money, but because Yidel knew no better way to be rid of them until they went to bed.

Ever since Chet's departure, the eldest ward was a girl called Naomie, whose parents, some said, were tree and wind: As an infant, she'd been found alone in the woods after a storm, and, over the decade since then, had grown up as tall and lanky as a white birch beneath a squall of black hair. Naomie was the only orphan Yidel could count on for the occasional copper. Envious, the other girls attributed this to witchcraft, and cursed her unnatural sylvan birth. Lecherous, the boys attributed it to prostitution, and cursed their own financial impotence. In truth, though, Naomie knew neither magic nor men. She was just like any orphan, a cast-off shadow of death.

For weeks, the gruel had been so meager that children were seasoning it with their own fingernails and earwax, when Naomie found, miraculously, in a basket on the orphanage doorstep, food enough to stretch a porridge for several days. The hidden patron must have been rich to have had such copious leftovers, and to let them go when they'd still do as feed or fertilizer. Probably a foreigner; the last generous local had been the sin-eater Ephraim.

By the time the others returned from their morning rounds, Naomie had prepared a feast that made even the widow Yidel wonder what incubus the girl had seduced. But who could utter a word when all mouths were full of food?

That night, Naomie dreamed that she'd killed a man she'd never seen before, bludgeoned him with a rock, and hauled him down to the river with a rope. The water was cold. She started to shiver. Waking in a fit of chill, she got up to see if the door was open. Through a break in the wood, she spied a man. Not the stranger she'd bludgeoned in her sleep. Someone as familiar as a brother. She watched as Chet dropped off another basket and left.

In the morning, she retrieved it, fuller even than the day before. With some rotten eggs and a slab of moldy cheese, she fried an omelet. She boiled a soup from a batch of chicken feet and six dried-up turnips. She was chopping up some mealy apples to bake a pie, when the other orphans started to arrive, sacks and cups as empty as their hollow bellies. They glared at her, as if she were to blame, but ate what she served them, and fought over the apples before she could put pie into oven.

Naomie's dream that night set her inside a mansion more extravagant than any she'd ever imagined. She was there alone with the miller, who had his arms around her, despite the fact that—she felt quite certain—she wasn't his wife. He kissed her. She recoiled onto the orphanage floor.

Before climbing back onto her straw mattress, Naomie looked out the door. She saw the basket, and then Chet walking away, his back to her.

He slept more soundly now that he had money. Within a few weeks of fortuitous deaths (an unscrupulous gambler, a farmer with a violent temperament), he'd collected enough to buy a small plot of land and to have a wooden cabin built on it. Most of the cabin was occupied by a great brick fireplace, where he warmed himself after his nightly rounds, and which he intended to set the scale for his future estate.

And already, by his estimation, he commanded more respect than old Ephraim: Moneylenders greeted him in the street, matchmakers offered him sturdy peasant girls with guaranteed dowries, and he even hired a chimney sweep, though his flue was still sootless. He also quietly engaged the services of an out-of-town tailor to fashion him a suit with hidden pockets, fit for a magician.

Into these he fed the victuals set out for him in the cemetery, vanishing comestibles with the alacrity he'd once dispatched mounds of granite, and extinguishing the death-watch candles with a rhetorical flourish. It was an elaborate performance, but the dead were said to be an unforgiving audience: He'd heard enough ghost stories not to want to imagine what would happen if the deceased believed he was bungling their atonement.

And he wasn't, not really. Chet was, by his own judgment, a moral alchemist, nourishing innocent orphans on sins committed before they were born, offering them not only daily sustenance but also the weight of history. If children inherit the flaws of their parents, the dead could become an orphan's surrogate family. Chet had it all figured out. His future was practically assured, the good life guaranteed, when, one night, he spied in the graveyard a set of open eyes.

Now it's a well-known fact that if a corpse meets your gaze you must not blink first, lest you be obliged to take the cadaver's place. (This is why the law requires sealed coffins and deep graves.) Cursing Ofer's negligence, Chet stepped forward to drop the dead lids. He reached out his hand into the receding night, but the vision passed like a specter: Nobody was there.

He might have dismissed the episode had the apparition been an aberration, but its sequel the next evening, and again the night after, led him to take precautionary measures. He set a trap. He dug a trench and covered it with twigs so fine that not even a hallucination could escape.

That evening, Naomie crept out of the orphanage just before midnight. She tiptoed down a side road, scurried into the woods. She scampered through trees under a moonless sky, as light and sure as a familiar. This was the place that had borne her, she'd been told for as long as she could remember, and she knew her way as certainly as other children recognized their mothers.

In a few minutes, she was at the cemetery gate, which she vaulted in a leap. Chet crouched. Hidden in the thicket of underbrush and tombstones, she edged forward through the generations. She stepped into her customary spot—and felt the ground take leave of her bare feet.

For a moment, Naomie stood atop a gap. Then she dropped, a six-foot plummet into a makeshift grave.

Chet rushed up to the pit, holding a candle and Ofer's spade. He peered over the lip as he threw in the first shovelful of dirt.

— What are *you* doing down there?

— What are you doing up *there*?

— I'm the town sin-eater. Everyone knows that, Naomie.

— You haven't been eating many sins lately.

Another load of dirt landed on her chest. Then one hit her in the face, hard, all rock and clod. The soil stuck where her nose began to bleed. She called his name, sharp like a sob.

— Chet, have you already forgotten that you were once an orphan like us?

— I remember the gruel all too well. You may be too proud to accept my charity, but I'll be damned if I lose a penny to your meddling.

— I've never told a soul your secret. I never will, Chet. I only wanted to understand the sins in my dreams.

— Why should I trust you? Why should I care? I'll give the food to vermin, and let the orphanage starve.

Naomie had climbed to her feet. She hoisted herself out of the pit, and came near to Chet. She hadn't seen him, except from afar, since he was a scrawny twelve-year-old boy whose fear of the widow Yidel marked him like the measles. He'd since become bulkier, to be sure, but the greater change had come about in his mouth, which glistened with greed. She shut her eyes and kissed him there, in the way she knew from her dreams. She let him fondle her, until he'd taken his pleasure.

He left her in naked pain. Yet only as her physical discomfort subsided did she begin to wonder whether the lingering mortification was the feeling of sin or of redemption.

Every night for many months she slipped into the cemetery and gave herself to the sin-eater, returning to the orphanage in the morning to make breakfast from the food he provided her. And Chet, he took home the cash. In short order, he was rich. He added so many rooms to his house that the fireplace had to be supplemented with three more. He bought his neighbors' land and tore down their hovels, to make room for a garden that would make the rabbi's Eden resemble a peasant's vegetable patch. He purchased animals fit for Noah's ark, clothing to match Joseph's coat, and a carriage to rival the Tabernacle.

A few of the town elders considered his pretensions unseemly, but everyone judged him an improvement over Ephraim: He negotiated his fees without so much fuss over family history, and dressed well at festivals. And what of penance? Given his success in business, who could question his skill at balancing the books in heaven?

He also, natural showman, mastered the extravagant gesture. He waived his sin-eating fees for the rabbi's relations, hosted banquets for visiting dignitaries, and, when the town hall needed repair, donated a new cupola. Granite to garnet, the orphan became a leading citizen—and the region's most eligible bachelor.

The matchmakers no longer bothered with sturdy peasant girls. They offered him burghers' daughters whose trousseaus came with chambermaids, and exotic beauties from islands too distant to have names. But nobody he met was right. The burghers' daughters came with attractive dowries, to be sure, and the exotic beauties promised to keep any man enchanted for a thousand and one nights or more. What did he want, then, the matchmakers asked. A princess? They located one for him, with blood so pure that, it was said, a single cut would drain the life from her. But he wouldn't be enticed, nor could he say why.

Chet asked Naomie to marry him. A full moon witnessed his proposal, and illuminated her response. Her eyes closed. She frowned. She said no.

He stood. He asked her if she knew what he owned, how much he had. She did. He said she couldn't possibly, unless she saw it all. He set her in the back of his carriage, and drove her to his estate. First they circled around his garden—which, unlike Eden, had flagstone roads laid for such excursions—naming for her the sleeping animals and flowers in the languages of their native lands. Then he brought her into his house, the foyer ceiling taller than the forest canopy, the halls more numerous than woodland trails, each leading to a bedroom, all of them empty except one, where he slept alone on silken sheets under blankets woven from gold thread. He led her there.

— Now you'll marry me.

— Anything else, Chet, but not that.

— You have nothing, Naomie.

— All I have, I've given you already.

— Then what have you got to lose? I don't expect a dowry. I've turned away dozens of those.

— I don't love you, Chet. I can't give you that. You can't buy it.

— Marry me anyway. You're the only one who knows me. The only one who's seen what I've done.

She let him hold her hands. She let him take her to bed. She let him caress her however he desired. She spent the whole night with him and when they awoke it was well past daylight.

He kissed her with that mouth that glistened with greed, and reiterated his vows. She shook her head and dashed back to the orphanage.

The others had, of course, noticed her empty cot, and, their suppositions confirmed, called her trollop and necromancer and succubus. Since she'd no bread with which to appease them this time, they didn't stop tormenting her even after Yidel sent them begging: In the sewer behind the orphanage, the boys molested her while the girls tore out her hair.

She was too ill to leave the orphanage that night. Chet waited for her in the graveyard. He waited 'til dawn, nibbling on sins as the hours passed and his hunger spread. When nothing was left, he slept.

Lately Chet's dreams had been as soft and warm as his bed, but, on this particular night, they raged through his head, angry and mean like a thrashing. At last Chet opened his eyes. He found Ofer standing over him, shouting his name.

— There's been a murder, Chet. The town bell has been ringing for hours.

— What concern is it of mine?

— The rabbi wants everybody to gather. Since you weren't at your estate, he sent me to fetch you here.

Hundreds of people were in the square, and still more were coming down every road. Chet looked for Naomie where the orphans stood. He couldn't find her. He tried to get closer, but the rabbi's disciples brought the meeting to order.

Sender appeared on the balcony of the town hall with the mayor, whom he'd single-handedly elected many years before, and whose only role was to stand beside the rabbi at municipal functions, lending them legitimacy in the capital city. Sender stepped forward and said that Reuven the moneylender had been murdered two nights before, and that his body was gone, save for a shroud of blood in his bed. The rabbi demanded a confession.

Of course nobody liked the moneylender, and almost all stood to have debts forgiven, or, rather, forgotten, now that he was gone, but no one was about to lay claim to the crime. Which presented a serious problem: With motivation nearly universal and the corporeal evidence gone missing, there was no means of investigation. Justice had to be done. Someone had to hang. The capital city insisted on it, and promised to handle it if the community couldn't. That meant large dogs and small cells from which folks didn't always emerge as whole as they'd entered: A town could be decimated by the time the crime was solved.

For three days, nobody came forward with a confession. In such situations there was but one course of action: Sender ordered Yidel's orphans to draw straws. Society has a use for everyone.

To ensure that Naomie's lot would be shortest, the children enlisted a boy named Falk, who was shrewdest at dice and cards and other games of chance, to hold the bundle while they drew. When Naomie's turn came, he spat in her eye so she wouldn't see him press down on the straw she was drawing, snapping it in two. If only Falk had been as good at addition as he was at division, his ruse would have worked. But he'd started with one lot too few, which left in his hands, when his own turn came, just the severed end of Naomie's straw. Anybody could see it was the shortest segment, that he'd botched the job. Everyone began talking at once, yet within a few moments, they'd reached a consensus: Naomie had used her witchcraft. Falk grabbed her straw, and, to universal approval, broke it to bits. Then they marched her to Sender, who imprisoned her in the town hall, and had his beadle post an announcement of her impending death.

When Chet went to the graveyard that night, he saw a copy of the notice. He read it twice. HANGING AT NOON, it said. ALL INVITED.

There were sins to be dispatched that evening, coins to be collected. He left the cemetery, though, candles still burning. He went to the rabbi's study.

As usual, Sender was with his disciples, reading through the night. When the pupils saw Chet coming, they surrounded the sin-eater, not to block his way, but to praise him, venerable citizen, and to admire his furs. Sender clapped his hands and waved for them to be gone. The disciples dispersed. The rabbi invited Chet inside, and poured him a cup of tea. The sin-eater took a sip. He set down his cup.

— Why are you punishing Naomie, Rabbi? She's innocent.

— She drew the shortest straw. You were in the orphanage once. You know how it works.

— But . . .

— Don't think of it as punishment, Chet. This has nothing to do with her personally.

— She's going to die.

— We have no other option.

For a moment, Chet thought about that. It wasn't right. The cheat stared at the rabbi.

— There's *me*.

— You haven't done anything wrong.

— *I'm* guilty.

The rabbi refused to believe him, so Chet went to the woods, where the remains of his former master still lay, and brought back some bones. He dropped them, one at a time, on Sender's floor. Did he give a showman's bow? The rabbi couldn't be sure.

— But those bones are old.

— Reuven wasn't a young man.

— What happened to the rest of him?

— Carrion.

— You wouldn't kill someone without a reason.

— I didn't like that he had as much money as me.

The rabbi wasn't convinced, but he had to admit that, at least from the standpoint of the capital city, Chet made a more compelling suspect than Naomie. Sender called for his beadle, who led the sin-eater to prison.

Naomie was stirred by the turning of the beadle's key. She opened her eyes. She squinted, perplexed. She stared at Chet. She murmured his name. She asked if he was her executioner. The beadle informed her that she was free. He said that she had to leave.

Only, she'd nowhere to go. The other orphans would already have parceled out her bedding, taken her place in the poorhouse. The streets were under curfew. She crept to the cemetery, where she figured Chet would go once he'd paid whatever bribes were behind her release. She curled up and slept. She dreamed of marrying him, of making children to fill each of his bedrooms.

The sun was nearly overhead when she woke again. All the candles had burned out. Vultures were consuming the sins. And Chet was still gone.

Then she heard the village bell tolling death, chiming in sets of thirteen. She tried to imagine how they were hanging her if she wasn't there. She tried to guess who they were executing in her place. Then she knew.

She plunged into the forest. She started to run. A root caught her foot. Her ankle snapped. Still she sprinted. She hit cobblestone. She broke through mobs of oglers into the hangman's procession. She saw Chet, bound in chains. She called out to the crowd. She said he couldn't possibly have killed Reuven, because on the night of the murder she'd been with him, in his bed. The mob ignored her, boastful little orphan girl. They wanted Chet dead: The cheat had never done anything except take their money and build himself a mansion. Had he ever actually atoned for the sins he purported to eat? Had he given alms? Ephraim had been holy. What was Chet? He was just greedy. The moneylender was forgotten, yesterday's murder, last week's villain. Chet was all they talked about, and he deserved nothing less than death.

Naomie turned from the crowd. Still shouting to be heard, she told Chet that she'd been wrong. She demanded to know how she could live without him, where she was supposed to go.

Was it gallows humor that made him mouth the word *graveyard*? A moment later, he was dead.

Not a soul attended Chet's funeral, except to pile waste atop his coffin, rancid animal offal and excrement, determined to bury him in his own sin. To complete the grotesque ritual, they surrounded his casket with every candle they could find in his house, lest his sins be carried away inadvertently by wild beasts.

The flame was furious. Terrified, Naomie hid inside a nearby crypt. The townsfolk went away. The sun set. At last she emerged, Naomie the orphan sin-eater. She approached her supper. As she got closer, the fire grew higher. It stretched past the treetops, each candle flame as broad as a trunk at the base, yet, up above, all of them branched together, woven into one light. She took another step. The fire collected. She plunged forward. The flame lifted, as if on a wind, and went out.

For many hours, Naomie was blind. Only with dawn did she see what had happened: The fire had consumed, completely, the food on Chet's coffin. There was no sin. Not a trace of who he'd been.

Naomie felt, deep in her stomach, a hunger unlike any she'd had before. And she knew that, no matter how much she ate, it would always be there. In that pit, she would always have Chet.

TET THE IDLER

Bell towers are the lighthouses by which we navigate the hours.

There once was a town with a clock that, like a bright beacon on the coastline, became a surrogate for the sun. Nobody ever rested in that town, for the bells rang all the time, a grand carillon that had been chiming, day and night, since before the eldest villagers were born. The townsfolk didn't question what caused the bells ceaselessly to repeat their song—whether it was a mechanical glitch or a metaphysical slip—any more than they wondered what it might be like to shut their eyes and sleep. Dreamy philosophy meant nothing to them. What mattered was that, on account of their peerless bell tower, their town prospered above all neighbors.

Folks worked constantly. Some farmed, while others plied the trades. But none toiled harder, under a greater burden, than Sol the timekeeper.

Sol was responsible for keeping the town clock wound. The carillon was powered by two lead weights, which ran down the center of the tower on loops of rope, and, if Sol wasn't hoisting one, he was tugging up the other. It was a job for two men, for which reason he'd heeded his father's deathbed advice: He'd taken a wife and raised a son.

The wife hadn't lasted many months past childbirth, but the son survived, as stout a boy as a papa could want. Sol called him Tet, and set him to work as soon as he could walk, fixing meals and cleaning up. Yet there wasn't much for a child, still too light to haul a weight, to do in a bell tower. While farmers and tradesmen always had suitable tasks for even their smallest sons and daughters, Tet had hours each day of leisure.

Some of these he spent watching folks work. He kept himself hidden, lest they solicit his help, for he knew that effort caused calluses and blisters, and wanted neither. He also saw that tireless exertion produced fine goods and delicate foods in such abundance that merchants from foreign lands were overwhelmed: If local builders weren't making new mills and kilns and looms, they were framing warehouses to store the surplus of luxuries ready for market.

When he wearied of seeing people toil—whether sowing or spinning or butchering cows, their jobs were as repetitive as the tower bells—Tet would visit the warehouses. There the boy could eat all the delicacies he wanted, wearing clothing woven of silk and gold, seated on a throne of cut gemstones. He'd pretend that he was the emperor of an exotic land, where everyone worked for his pleasure. If he wore a fur mantle, he envisioned a manservant wrapping him in it. If he ate a crown of figs or a round of cheese, he pictured a maid bringing it to him on a golden platter. His maids always had ample breasts and his men were sturdy like livestock. He couldn't imagine a finer retinue, yet, no matter what he had them do for him, his fantasies felt a bit empty: There was nobody to enjoy his leisure with him.

It was not for want of effort on his part. A hundred times he tried to come up with conversations to detain the servants in his reveries. A thousand times, he contemplated ruses to befriend them. But like the people he watched in field and shop, those who populated his fictions were beholden to the carillon. He simply didn't know how to dream up folks who weren't.

Tet asked his father why nobody ever used the luxuries that the town produced.

— Those goods are sold.

— Who buys them?

— Merchants. You know that, Tet. You've seen them come in with their lorries and haul away all that they can carry. You see them practically every week.

— Then what do they do with all the goods they get? Do *they* use them?

— They barter the goods. That's what makes them merchants.

— They barter the goods with people who use them?

— They barter the goods with other merchants.

— And *those* merchants . . . ?

— Can't you see I'm busy? Why do you care? Why aren't you upstairs, polishing the carillon bells, Tet? You know the chime must be bright. You know the town depends on that.

— But when the merchants take away our goods, what do we get?

— They give us credit. That's what makes us the richest town in the kingdom. It's why we're admired.

Tet didn't ask more. He climbed the height of the tower. The carillon song rang in his ears as he stood beneath the swaying bells, polishing rags piled at his feet. He surveyed the landscape, stacked high with industry set inside a garland of lush farmland. The warehouses were beyond the farms, clustered on a crest above the stone quarries. The rest was uncut forest, through which ran roads traveled by merchants to villages known to Tet only through legend. He'd heard that they were desperately behind the times, these realms, that their bells rang but once a day. He peered down the belfry at his father, a knot of musculature toiling away the years. Tet tried to picture himself in Sol's place, but he could envision it even less than the most outlandish of his warehouse fantasies. He yawned. He was bored. By the time his father called up to ask how the polishing was coming, he'd already slipped away.

Nobody saw Tet for a while after that. Folks didn't speak of it, any more than they discussed the ways of rivers or stars. He was known to be a loafer, inalterable, spared rod or exile only out of deference to his father.

Maybe a day went by, possibly two or more, before a laborer passing from one task to another happened upon the boy's body, sprawled out under a tree where the forest began at the edge of town. The laborer called out to others. Cluster heaped to crowd. Questions tossed around. Was Tet mauled by a bear? Slain by a thief? His body bore no mark of death. Soft and fair, Tet appeared barely to have been touched by life.

Then somebody saw his eyes open. The crowd drew back. They knew the look of a demon, that species of dybbuk the size of a human soul, that takes possession of the dead as a comestible home. This one was peering out the windows of its new abode. The crowd shuddered. The body stiffened. Its mouth opened. *Where am I? What happened to me?*

Tet staggered to his feet. He stared at the ground where he'd lain. He stirred the dirt with his foot. Then he turned around and asked the mob what had become of the town.

— The town is fine.

— Why is everyone here, then?

— This is where we found you. This is where you died.

— But I think that I'm alive.

— It will probably pass. A moment ago, you were flat on your back.

Tet didn't remember. All that he recalled was walking out

to the woods, as he occasionally did, sitting under a tree, and watching time go by. He found that it moved faster if he closed his eyes, like an unwatched pot coming quicker to boil, but what had happened in this instance was most unusual: He'd shut his eyes and the day had simply vanished.

Some of the older peasants remained wary, but on the whole it was agreed that, if he could stand, he could work, and that was the only criterion anyone had when it came to questions of life and death. He walked back to town with several laborers and climbed up the bell tower, where he renewed his efforts on the carillon, polishing the brass with rags. A *miracle,* folks said of him. A *resurrection.* Then they returned to their cattle and forges and ovens.

Tet, on the other hand, was only beginning to reckon where he'd been. As he skirted around the pealing bells, he recollected a landscape quite unlike the one reflected in the trembling metal. The hills had all been in their customary places, as had the river that powered the mills, yet none of the great waterwheels had been there to turn stream into machine, and the forest had lapsed all the way down to the shore. Tet did remember seeing some buildings, most particularly the tower where he was presently standing, yet broken down with weeds growing up within. Most haunting of all, though, had been the quiet, the total absence of people. He went to his father.

— Where do folks go when they aren't here?

— Nobody in this town ever abandons his duties, Tet, not even for a moment. When you grow up, you won't either. It's time you learned that this isn't a place for idlers.

Tet tried to work harder. He made the bells so shiny that he could see the sun dizzy with envy. But nothing shimmers as persistently as curiosity. As day fell to night, Tet again abandoned clock tower for forest floor.

He sat down to think things over. Not being very thoughtful, his mind soon wandered.

At last he saw the sun rising. He bade it good morning, for he didn't wish it to begrudge him his work in the bell tower. His voice sounded unusually loud to him, the only noise in the valley. He listened. The carillon was not ringing.

He hurried into town. Naked brick chimneys stood cold, stripped of their surrounding shops. The marketplace was a field of nettles. He kept walking. He went in the direction from which merchants often came. He took the road many miles, all the way to the next village.

By then, the sun was in its prime. Somewhere a clock struck twelve times. People crowded the streets, speaking to one another in terms so strange that he forgot he knew the language.

Folks are such gossips, he heard a girl declare. Since that was a profession with which he wasn't familiar, he turned to her. Her soft body was too large a bounty for the coarse hemp dress she wore, and, were her blond pigtails less full—falling forward over broad shoulders—her breasts might have been deemed indecent. *And what,* she said, staring back at Tet, *are you looking at?*

He took a guess. *A gossip?* he said.

The girl laughed, he wasn't sure why, but she seemed to take a liking to him, which was more than any other girl had done. She glanced at his broad chest, and then at his face, so unblemished under a first growth of beard that he might have been a squire. She asked him where he came from. He named his town.

— You're teasing me.

— It doesn't look like much now, but not long ago it was bigger than your village. It was a commercial center.

— My father once told me about that place. He said it's a town where nobody sleeps.

— What's sleep?

— You don't know? You poor man. I think you may be telling me the truth. Sleeping is what you're doing now.

Tet was more confused than he'd ever been. He wished he'd

never started the conversation. Even polishing the carillon was easier than understanding what she said. Then the girl took his hand, and he knew that he'd follow her anywhere.

She didn't take him far, simply brought him to where she lived, the loft of the barn where she worked as a milkmaid. When they climbed the ladder, she pointed at the hay stacked in the corner.

— That's a bed. It's where people go to sleep.

— I see. How does it work?

— When you aren't teasing me, you're trying to seduce me.

She sighed. At least he was more handsome than her peasant boyfriends. She lay down, reached up a hand, and pulled him on top of her.

For all his hours among silks and furs, Tet had never encountered luxury such as this girl's flesh. She helped him to empty her out of her sackcloth dress. He gathered the abundance of her breasts. She laughed at him, and, while teaching him to kiss, ripped open his britches. Neither was prepared for the quickness with which the next lesson came, for it was new to both of them.

They didn't speak for several minutes. There was just the mutual give-and-take of breath. Then Tet asked the girl to marry him.

— Marry you? Where would we go?

— I like it in bed.

— Nobody sleeps all the time, silly. If you married me, you'd have to bring me home to your town.

— I'll bring you wherever you want to go. I'll take you to my town right now.

— You expect me to live in a pile of rubble?

— It's a nice place when you're awake.

He looked at her. He saw that he'd have to do better. He vowed to give her the town of her dreams.

Reluctantly, he dressed and returned home. He returned to

the broken-down clock tower. The carillon had collapsed within. He attempted to lift it, but of course he couldn't. He found a rag and started to polish. The cloth disintegrated in his hand. What could be done? How to begin? There was nothing where the shops had been, except more disrepair. Forget silks and gold. The town wanted iron and wood and stone. Tet wandered in despair. He sat beneath a tree. He shut his eyes. He had an idea.

Two lumberjacks, young brothers, were clearing forest together—timbering trees in time with the carillon—when a corpse startled them from their labors. From their mother, they'd heard about Tet's miraculous resurrection, yet here he was, dead again. Their mother had said that, if he wasn't the devil, he must be very holy. They bowed their heads, and, after a spell, heard a voice address them: *If you'll follow me, I'll show you a forest much greater than this.*

Then Tet started to describe where he'd been, explaining that there was a realm of dreams as vast as the land in which they stood, yet neglected for many unslept centuries by their countrymen: a village fallen to ruin, rimmed with unharvested timber, awaiting rediscovery. By the time his story was done, night had come, and they were seated on the ground. He urged the brothers to shut their eyes. And soon they saw all that he had said.

In their dreams, they chopped down oaks stouter than oxen. They were strong men, and together they landed enough trees to build a mill, if only they'd a capable carpenter on hand to build it. A carpenter like their cousin. The moment they awoke, they left Tet to enlist him.

On that particular day, the carpenter happened to be enlarging one of the sawmills on the river, tooling it to finish an acre of lumber each hour. The brothers told him that they needed him to frame a mill for them: They'd provide the timber, he'd be their partner, and, where they planned to build, there was no competition. The novelty of opportunity made them dance around him like children.

In all his years, he'd never seen such zeal, let alone felt it himself. He asked where they'd been. They had him lie down and shut his eyes. They did the same. And, all together, their dreamwork was resumed.

In the weeks that followed, word of Tet's discovery gained ground. For the young, it was as if he'd found a new world, one that they themselves could conceive and build. Older folks were less enthusiastic. They'd been willing to overlook Tet's selfishness when he kept it to himself, but to implicate others in his lazy ways was outright seditious. His followers insisted that he worked harder than anybody, for the greater good, supervising their dreams and recruiting new labor while they were awake. All that the older generation saw, though, was a sham miracle worker who'd staged a humbug resurrection to spread mass delusion. On Tet's account, the young were working merely twelve hours a day, halving village productivity. Surely a law was being broken, even if it had yet to be written. An inquisition was called, held under the clock tower out of deference to loyal Sol, who wouldn't abandon the bells, he said, just to witness his son's execution.

The trial began. The burghers refused to admit as evidence anything that couldn't be brought in front of them. Tet's supporters urged the old men to shut their eyes, to see what lay behind. The burghers jeered: Tet may lead a young fellow by the chin, but justice isn't blind.

Put in those terms, by men of wealth and prestige, Tet's enterprise no longer looked so plausible to his faction. One by one, they aligned themselves with the burghers. They urged Tet to recant, and to go back to work for his father: If only he were useful, the town would never waste him on a principle.

— I made a promise.

— First you're making mills. Now you're making promises. Who's going to believe it?

— I proposed to a girl from the next village.

— No one will ever marry you, Tet. All you ever do is loaf.

— She accepted, provided that I make our town a pleasant place to sleep. But now I wouldn't bring her here, no matter what I vowed. This town isn't even a good place to be awake.

At a nod from the head burgher, the lumberjack brothers hauled Tet toward the jail. They reached the steps, where a benighted crone stood in their path. She was as ingrown as an old vine, and as rooted to the ground. The woman was grandmother to several of the burghers, and a great-aunt to many others. Calling them to her, quieting them down, she urged Tet to describe his sleep again. She permitted nobody to interrupt. When Tet was done, she put her hands on his shoulders, and said that, when she was a girl, her grandfather had described something similar, which she'd always thought was mere fable: In his childhood, the bell tower had chimed on the hour, and folk had spent half their time in slumber. Then a terrible storm had come, a black wind, and everything had changed. Folks had no longer found time to dream. The carillon had developed a chronic case of insomnia. Over the years, people grew accustomed to their condition, conditioned to custom. Such things happen. The dream space of prior generations became foreign to the town, beyond the reach of imagination.

A delegation of three burghers was immediately appointed to explore Tet's dreams. Three beds of straw were made. When the sun set, the men shut their eyes. And found themselves looking out on a town like their own in another time. They glanced at one another, agape at the potential of such undeveloped real estate. Half-built, the shops stood empty, and the farmland had not been partitioned yet. They mounted the steps of the clock tower, still uncrowned by a carillon, and surveyed the uncut forest, calculating its commodity value by the acre. The numbers were too unwieldy even for all three of them together to handle. It was just as well. None wanted to admit his debt to Tet, let alone share with the others the potential wealth.

For hours, folks watched the three sleeping burghers, elderly men, well bearded and full-bellied. In their slumber, the men began to snore. They sounded like pigs at a trough. Fearful of what was happening—that their dreams were corrupting them—their wives shook them awake. For a moment, the men looked lost. Then they were talking, all three at once, to establish who owned what.

Nobody listened to their haggling. While the burghers quibbled through the night, beneath the chiming carillon, the town went to sleep.

Over the next three months, a little each night, the town was rebuilt under Tet's watch. Shops were enclosed and occupied by craftsmen, who began to ply their trades as they did while awake. Fields flourished under horse and plow. Most dramatic, though, was the effect of this dual citizenship on the populace: Because neither wakefulness nor sleep was absolute, each put the other into perspective. Each could accommodate idleness as well as work. Each was a refuge from the other, and a respite.

Tet didn't take credit for that, though admiration for his enlightened stewardship naturally netted many marriage offers. In one dream, there was even a call to make him mayor. He declined the honor: His job was in the bell tower, ensuring that it rang on the hour, neither less often nor more.

His father refused to follow such a sensible plan. Sol would not sleep in the bed that Tet made for him, nor would he permit any adjustment to his clockwork. He didn't believe in dreams, no matter what folks told him. He alone stood awake at night, chiming perpetual noon for no one.

Only in that respect was Tet's vow unfulfilled, and the town not yet suitable for his betrothed. He argued and begged, but still the old man would not relent.

At last he set out to fetch his fiancée anyway. In his dream, he roamed from farm to farm. He found her barn. She was inside, just where he'd left her, only much rounder than he'd remembered.

She motioned him close. She lifted her dress and brought his face to her belly. She ran her hands through his beard, and murmured, *Our baby.*

Then she let Tet kiss her, and hire a carriage to take her away. With help from the coachman, he carried her down from the hayloft and up into the covered hack.

All the way home, Tet told her about his town, introducing her by description to everyone. Finally he got to his father.

He won't sleep, my papa. He tends to the carillon all night long. It rings and rings and rings, and he believes nothing.

— You haven't told him about me?

He calls you my hallucination.

— As the months went by, I was beginning to think that you were mine.

They kissed again, more deeply, emerging from their embrace to find themselves in the middle of his town. Tet emerged from the carriage. The square was abandoned. He began to stammer that the people must be elsewhere.

The girl laughed at him. She pointed at the clock tower.

— Don't be ridiculous. It's time to wake up, Tet.

— But we just got here.

— Open your eyes. You can't dream forever.

For several minutes, Tet struggled to stay asleep, to remain with her. He fought ground and sky into a blur. He went blind.

As he opened his eyes, he saw the carriage riding away. He tried to chase after it. The square was too crowded. Crowded with people gazing in his direction. Behind him, he heard ringing. Was it the carillon? It was a voice, singing out his name.

He turned. First he saw the burghers. Then he saw his father, come down from the bell tower, struck, at last, by tangible truth: Old Sol stood with the other elders behind the girl, whose dress, stretched taut against her swollen belly, shone white in the morning light. She was laughing. She was calling to Tet. She was calling him to their wedding.

YOD THE INHUMAN

When the scholar Meir lost his wife of twenty years, he did not hire the town matchmaker to find him another. Instead he collected mud from the bed of a river, hauled it home, and sculpted it into a girl on the floor of his cellar.

Meir had studied anatomy, and worked every muscle and sinew into the cold clay more accurately than had ever been achieved in a statue. He'd also studied art, and slimmed the girl's waist narrower, and opened her eyes wider, than had ever been accomplished by nature. Into each empty socket, he set a star sapphire. Then he pricked his finger, and drew with his blood the cipher for life that he'd once seen inscribed in an ancient holy book.

The figure began to breathe. In the candlelight, he saw that her skin was tawny like the clay, and her hair was darkest umber, yet, when he beckoned her, he felt nothing loamy to her touch. By morning, she was his mistress.

Meir gave her his wife's old clothes to wear, and the dead woman's wooden brush, so that the girl might keep the sign on her forehead—that enchanting birthmark—always hidden beneath her hairline. He also gave his mistress a name, by which to obey him. He called her Yod.

In almost every respect, Yod was an improvement over Meir's wife, with whom he'd fought constantly since the day their marriage was arranged. Henye had come from a family with servants, and she'd had no wish to become one herself, but her husband hadn't accepted a position in her father's business, as expected: He'd kept to his scholarship rather than becoming a shipping clerk, and, her whole dowry spent on inexplicable books, she'd been left to cook the meals and mop the floors. That, at least, had been her point of view.

In Meir's opinion, his wife had performed every task inadequately, squandering the pennies he made as a scribe and translator—money earned at the expense of his studies—on flour she could have milled or meat she could have butchered or wood she could have timbered, with her own two hands. When she'd reminded him that she was a cripple, clubfooted since birth, he'd retorted that she'd hidden that well enough while she was in the market for a husband, so it couldn't be too serious an affliction.

Naturally there were no such faults with Yod, who did what Meir asked of her instantly, without thinking to quibble. Because she hadn't any needs of her own, all work was the same, and she'd tirelessly keep at it until told to stop. In his house, his rule was absolute, and, within those four walls, he faced the predicament of princes: The totality of Yod's subservience demanded that he know exactly what he wanted.

With practice, he got good at that. And his satisfaction with her would have been complete, were it not for the least expected of flaws: Meir had trouble taking pleasure in his mistress.

With her clubfoot and hairy chin, his wife had not especially attracted him, nor had his bowlegged scholar's body and urine-blond froth of beard particularly moved her erotically, yet when they'd gotten down to it, shared hatred had enflamed them, and they'd fought their way to ecstasy. Meir had none of that with Yod. In bed she let him do to her whatever he wished. She consented without comment to acts he'd never have contemplated with Henye, and granted without complaint every favor he asked of her. She was as selfless at copulation as she was at cooking and mopping. But the more of his expectations she met, the less satisfied he felt. Every night before he put her to rest by rubbing the mark of life from her forehead, he gazed at her wide sapphire eyes and tight tawny waist, and wondered what could possibly be wanting. And, every morning, when he pricked his finger and reinscribed the vital sign on her still, clay figure, he pondered how she could conceivably not fulfill his desires.

Because Meir no longer took work as a scribe or translator, and Yod fetched his wood and water, he seldom spoke to other people anymore. But he did have one old acquaintance: He and the village rabbi, Selig, had once been schoolmates.

They were as different as two men could be. Plump and gregarious, the rabbi had a biblically large family that crowded his home, and defined his life, as fully as Meir's was informed by his library. That Selig had no books didn't concern folks. At school he would have flunked without Meir's Talmudic expertise, yet here he was town maggid—while Meir was ignored—because Selig was blessed with common sense.

He received Meir with a ripe kiss on each cheek and a deracinating embrace, while unwashed grandchildren clutched at the fringes of the scholar's gown. He offered Meir tea, and, when his guest demurred, proposed a walk along the river. He ushered the scholar through a thicket of untended garden, out into the open. They traveled in silence along the river, through croft and meadow, until at last the rabbi asked whether Meir intended to marry the golem he'd made.

— What makes you call Yod a golem?

— Because she is one. A girl like that doesn't just appear on her own. In town, they're calling you a sorcerer.

— Then others also know about her? Did you tell them?

— They told me, Meir. They saw a stranger with star sapphire eyes and tawny skin draw water from the well, half her weight to the bucket, and watched where she brought it. If you ever left your books for a minute, you'd hear them talking. The men are hoarse with envy.

— They shouldn't be. She works hard, and you see how she looks, but that isn't all a man wants.

— She isn't a good lover. What did you expect, Meir? The girl is made of mud.

— She follows all of my orders.

— A golem will. The point is, she can't feel.

Meir hadn't considered that, for psychology was one field that he had not studied. The rabbi wrapped a hand around the scholar's stooped shoulders, content to have solved his problem. He didn't mind that Meir was quiet again as they walked back to town. He took it to mean that this whole vexing golem business had been laid to rest.

Yet Meir's silence was not calm: Selig hadn't cured his affliction, but merely diagnosed it for him. He declined the rabbi's supper invitation. He extracted himself from Selig's farewell embrace. As the sun went down, he scurried home to Yod, for he knew what had to be done.

That was the night of Yod's first lesson. Meir began by showing her pain, because it seemed less ambiguous than pleasure, more fundamental. In bed, he pinched her flesh. *Hurt,* he said.

Hurt, she repeated, expressionless.

He pinched her harder, on the neck. *Hurt,* he said, louder.

Hurt, she mimicked, and smiled.

He slapped Yod hard across the mouth. He cursed her stupidity. He flipped her onto her belly, pulled her dress up over her rump, and relieved himself inside her numb slot. As he clutched her head to rub her out, she murmured. The word she exhaled, in a voice he'd never before heard, was *hurt*.

For several days after that, he ravaged her body with every form of torture he could conjure—*bruise, blister, burn*—to foster the broadest possible understanding of pain. Then he sought to show her pleasure.

At first, she was too tender. She could speak only of hurt, no matter how Meir handled her. But every hour that he stroked her hair, whispering *calm* in her ear, she trembled less with terror.

She began coming to him between chores, laying her head on his lap, and burbling *calm* in her contralto singsong. He gave her kisses, which she learned to *yearn*. From that came naturally the urge that, in her fervid clutch, he told her was *lust,* but which she pronounced *love*.

Pleasure changed Yod more than pain. She wasn't always obedient anymore. She had her own cravings. When Meir didn't give her the affection she expected, she sat in a chair and pouted, and, if he threatened punishment, she struck first and hit hardest. Every night, he was exhausted by her. Her passion bruised and blistered and burned. In pain, he began to question the wisdom of teaching a golem to feel. But Meir was too weary to see the rabbi or even to look up the matter in his books. And then one evening, after she'd extracted from him every dribble of desire, he fell asleep without blotting her forehead cipher.

Yod had never seen a man dormant. Her master wasn't at all pleasurable like that. After waiting an eternity, perhaps several minutes in duration, for Meir to revive, she climbed out of bed, and opened the door. Outside, the moon was full. Its glow felt like a cool slip over her bare skin. Yod shivered. Whispering her words—*hurt* and *calm* and *love*—and gathering them under her tongue again for safekeeping, she stepped into the night, seeking feeling.

In Meir's dreams, he couldn't move because his flesh was mud. When he awoke, his whole body was frigid. Through the predawn dim, he saw that his door was open. Then a deeper chill beset him: His girl was gone.

Dashing into the street, his shabby robes still open, he tried to determine who'd broken into his home: What man in his town would attempt such a bold theft? Then he rephrased the question: To possess his Yod, who wouldn't?

He accosted the first folks he met, a clutch of drunken farmhands stumbling down the steps of the village tavern. He stood in front of them, blocking their path.

— Did any of you steal my girl?

— Steal her? She gave herself to us.

— She wouldn't. You have her, then?

— We sent her away when we were done. We banged your girl good, Meir, but she wanted more men.

— You're lying. You know I'll have you beaten.

The laborers looked at one another. They knocked him down, kicked him into the gutter, and buried him in laughter.

After a spell, Meir rolled himself over, roused by an odor stronger than smelling salts. The beggar Issachar was leaning over him, wondering if he was hurt. Meir staggered to his feet, mumbling about having stumbled on a loose paving stone. Then he asked if the beggar had perchance been up all night. Issachar nodded his hooded head; he couldn't afford to rest. The scholar asked if he'd seen Yod.

— The girl with tawny skin and star sapphire eyes? I was just with her.

— With her? What do you mean? Where?

— Behind the tavern in the alley. She begged me. I couldn't turn her away. How often does a beggar have a chance to give?

— You raped her.

The scholar lunged at Issachar, but the beggar's stench—guardian angel of tramps—knocked Meir back into the gutter. Issachar did not laugh at him, nor did he run. The beggar simply stood his ground. At last, Meir apologized. Climbing to his feet again, he asked where Yod had gone. Issachar unfolded a finger, long and crooked. He pointed toward the woods.

Of course Meir was learned enough to know that the forest was where evil thoughts fled as imps and sprites to become full-grown demons, and that even a golem couldn't long withstand their nocturnal torments. He headed for his library, but wound up, agitated beyond reckoning, at the house of the rabbi.

Selig was still in bed, smothered in children, regaling them with old folktales while they giggled and stole sips of sweet tea from his chipped cup. Meir's appearance stilled them. They stared at him—a man beaten and broken like a wretch from their grandfather's legends—and scrambled.

Selig gently grasped his hand. He pulled Meir close and quietly observed that the scholar had not followed his advice.

— But I did. I made Yod feel.

— I don't think that was my suggestion. You know I'm not a clever man. Tell me what happened.

The scholar gave him a thorough accounting. He omitted nothing.

— Then you're free of her.

— *Free* of her? I *need* her.

— There's plenty of mud by the river. If you're so desperate for a mistress, why not make another?

— She wouldn't be Yod.

— That depends on what you name her.

— You don't understand, Selig. I made her feel.

— You made her *feel*? You're in love, Meir. There's nothing to be done, unless you're prepared to pursue her.

For all his erudition, the scholar could not find fault in what the rabbi said, and, in his desperate state, the alternate solution that he found in his books—burying the girl's name in an unmarked grave—seemed downright ludicrous. That morning, he pawned his library and took a loan in gold against his home. From a peddler, he bought a cart horse with legs more bowed than his own, and, after several failed attempts to mount her, hobbled through town on the old nag's back. Everyone stopped to taunt him, the Kabbalah-conjurer who held himself so high and mighty above them, only to be cuckolded by his own golem. They threw rotten fruit and clots of dirt, and made such lewd remarks about Yod that Meir wondered who—man, woman, or child—hadn't molested her.

The forest was so vast that the demons spoke seven different dialects. Some lived in the trees, sailing on the winds, while others were subterranean and blind. Obviously, their cultures also differed. The largest were beasts of destruction, ground-dwelling brutes who'd fell whole civilizations and foul themselves when they were done. The slightest of them, airborne wisps as gentle as dust, thrived on deception, sweeping societies with rumor and prejudice, high on their own delusion. But neither of these demons concerned people much: The workings of natural disaster were too calamitous, and of human nature too ubiquitous, for folks to address. Theft and rape and murder, on the other hand, were demons of a scale that everybody could grasp, and in many countries bordering on the forest, princes offered a bounty on such evils. Peasants would band together after dark, significantly decreasing the local crime rate, even if no demons were actually caught.

Folks learned to season their vigilance with cunning. They set traps and lay in wait. And one night, in a small principality where river met sea, some old peasants made a catch.

While not exactly beastly, the creature clearly was no ordinary girl. Sprawled on the ground, stark naked, bleeding where the trap clasped her ankle, she stared at her captors through star sapphire eyes, mouthing the word *hurt*.

The language she spoke was foreign to them. They suspected that it might be a hex. They gagged her and bound her in rope. To the palace, they dragged her through the dirt. They hollered for their prince. They called for their reward.

The prince met them in the courtyard. The farmers tipped their hats as His Majesty approached, but they did not lower their voices. Each shouting to be heard over the rest, all of them tried to impress the young royal with how courageous they'd been to capture such a demon. When the prince saw the girl lying at their feet, though, he no longer heard their boasts. He got down on his knees like a commoner, to untie her.

He broke through the knots with strong hands. The peasants looked on in horror. Did His Majesty know the danger of releasing such a fierce beast within the palace gates?

— She isn't a demon.

— She came from the forest. You can be sure she is one.

— Look at her slender waist, her wide eyes. She's probably an abducted princess. A girl like this could get taken up by the devil himself.

She shivered. The prince wrapped his own velveteen robe around her bare shoulders. He asked her where she came from. When she didn't respond, he surmised that she must be an exotic princess indeed, and led her to his chambers to investigate further. The peasants demanded their bounty. The prince replied that if anyone ever again called her unnatural, their reward would be the gallows.

The next day, His Majesty announced that he was marrying

her. His courtiers, many of them old enough to remember the day his father married his noble mother, and most of whose daughters had been his mistresses on the basis of princely promises, wanted to see her credentials. They asked from what court she'd been abducted. Touching her tawny skin, he deemed her pedigree Arabian or African. They demanded to know her name. Turning his royal back, he said that they could address her as Your Majesty when they met her the following morning at his wedding.

Yod, of course, had never before been bathed in rose water. She'd never had her hair woven into a hundred sinuous braids, laced with strands of seed pearl, and she'd never been stitched into a gown of fresh magnolia petals, embroidered with polli- nated thread. Yet almost every incident in her brief life had been unprecedented. She hadn't the experience to know sur- prise. As the prince set her with his finest gems—clusters of di- amonds around her neck, crystal crown upon her head—he was reassured that he'd chosen his wife well: To carry such magnifi- cence so lightly, he surmised, her gentle blood must flow back, unobstructed, to the Garden of Eden.

Watching her saunter down the palace steps in slippers of gold leaf, even his haughtiest courtiers laid their nobility humbly at her feet, in deepest bows and curtsies. They all lis- tened as the prince exchanged vows with his betrothed. Yod pronounced her words precisely as he'd taught her. She didn't yet know what they meant, but when she kissed him, her lips expressed perfectly how she felt.

For many months after that, the prince wasn't seen except with his princess. They shared his throne, and together wielded his scepter, for their fingers were always entwined. The arrangement suited his subjects: Considering them no differ- ent from herself, the princess embraced their concerns with trusting fervor. They adored her openly, honoring her with garlands of fresh flowers each day—and every night, behind closed doors, she quenched her husband's jealousy.

And how he sated her! Every pleasure that old Meir had promised, that he'd urged her to yearn, her young husband provided, and desired in kind. In his hands, his wife softened. Her tawny skin warmed. Her sapphire eyes burned.

Yet a golem, even a royal one, lacks human perception. Yod didn't notice, less than a year into her marriage, the flicker in her husband's gaze when he looked at courtiers' newly adolescent daughters, nor did she discern meaning in their giggling when, for misbehavior that mystified her, he called them to the throne for a spanking.

Then he decreed that, as an anniversary gift, his dear princess would spend a month at his country's famed rejuvenating baths.

— You need a rest.

— I'm very happy in your bed.

— You don't want to lose your youth.

— I'm not as fresh as I used to be?

— You have wrinkles behind your knees.

— Doesn't everyone?

— Don't contradict me. Are you trying to be ugly?

Yod shook her head. The prince patted her on the chin. But when she sought his mouth, he turned his shoulder.

The dress she wore for her voyage, a whole garden of orchids woven together at the stem, was more glorious even than her wedding gown. Her hair was braided with ribbons of gold leaf, and her tiara was cut from a single slice of lapis. In her open carriage, traveling through the countryside with her ten-car entourage, she embodied the prince's prestige—reminding the peasants of his palatial majesty—and the courtiers he sent to watch over her would have made much of the occasion had the princess not looked so sickly. The flowers wilted on her feverish body, and her crown weighed so heavily on her head that, when she stood, she had to be held up by two chambermaids. By the time Yod got to the sanatorium, she needed one.

The baths could accommodate a hundred women and men, yet, to protect Her Majesty's highborn modesty, the facility was given to her alone. Early each morning, she was packed in cool mud, which dried in the sun until noon. Then she was steeped in hot springs until dusk, and soaked in cold baths until she could count a thousand stars above. At last, to take in the air, she was put to bed on a hammock, so exhausted that her dreams were a blur. In those nightmares, she couldn't distinguish between pain and pleasure, nor could she tell whether the man administering it was the prince or Meir.

The thirty days and thirty nights passed, ripples in the ancient baths. On the final morning, the fields were filled with daisies, newly in blossom. Yod sent her maids to fetch as many as they could carry. With her own fingers, she tied them in a chain, and wrapped them around her body until she'd made a dress. The handful she had left, she linked together in a tiara.

The courtiers, who scorned such common flowers, had other ideas about how she ought to be attired. They brought out strands of rubies and emeralds from treasure chests as large as wardrobes. They reminded her that, after all, she was a princess. *Just so,* she said, *I'll wear what I please.*

She sat high in her carriage, anticipating how her husband would embrace his bride in full bloom, never again letting her out of his sight. She passed through the palace gate. Trumpets sounded. Nobles gathered. Only nowhere in their midst did she see the prince.

Before she could ask questions, she was ushered to a banquet to celebrate her return, seated at the end of a long table. All the way at the opposite end, past legions of gentry, His Majesty reclined, a young girl on each side. The princess recognized them, two sisters, twin daughters of his bursar, whose giggling naughtiness had merited them great fits of spanking by His Majesty in the weeks before the prince sent Yod away. She watched his gaze shift back and forth between them, identically plump and blond and hazel-eyed, and, while she could appreciate their need for discipline—they ate with their fingers from His Majesty's plate, and whispered in his ears with their mouths full, wiping their greasy hands clean on his velveteen gown—she didn't understand why their father never glanced in their direction, nor why personal responsibility for their supervision should fall to her husband. Yet whenever she sought to catch his attention, to remind him that she was home, one of the twins would tap on his shoulder or tug on his ear, and a matron sitting near Yod would inquire about her mud bath regimen.

She was obliged to describe her days over and over again, and by the nineteenth time, the prince had slipped away. The hour was late. The table was cleared. And still the women held Yod in conversation. She yawned. She announced that she was going to bed. They asked if she planned evermore to sleep in a hammock. *Never again,* she declared, and wouldn't be detained by their banter for a moment longer.

Straight to her husband's chambers Yod went. The door was shut. Behind it she heard a loud moan, and then another, much softer. Her hand fell on the latch. When it didn't give, she broke it, and entered.

The prince had both twins in bed with him. The one named Raina clutched his scepter. The one named Raisa wore his crown. And, in the light of a single white wax candle, both glistened with his semen.

Without a word of explanation, His Majesty turned his back on Yod. The girls, though, climbed out of bed and, brash in their naked white flesh, strutted up to the princess. Raina plucked a petal from her daisy-chain dress and twittered, *He loves me.* Raisa yanked a petal and warbled, *He loves me not.* They started to giggle, and within a minute had her stripped of every petal—taunting *loves me, loves me not*—leaving only an uncomely tangle of stems on her murky skin.

For a while, Yod did not move. She watched the twins slip back into bed with her husband, caressing him with each other's breasts, and moaning in his ears, until he was moved to mount them again. She watched as all three forgot about her, and then she staggered out the door.

Several of her maids were waiting there. As she fainted, they caught her, and carried her off to bed.

Yod slept for a week. When she awoke, the prince was standing by her pillow. He informed her that she had to get dressed, for that evening there was a pageant to celebrate their anniversary. She tried to ask about the twins, unsure of what, in her delirium, she had seen.

— You're my princess. My subjects expect to see you with me.

— And the bursar's daughters?

— Don't you worry about them. They know their place. Concern yourself with yours.

He left her to be bathed and gowned and coiffed and crowned. At dusk he took her hand at the palace gate, and walked her to the royal coach. Together they rode through the streets at the head of a noble procession. At every turn, folks called out to her, for she was still a most popular princess, beloved by all—except, so it seemed, her husband.

For the length of their excursion, she wasn't once able to speak to him, to make herself heard over the celebration of their first year of connubial bliss. And then it was done, carriage returned to the stables and husband hustled off by minions. She might have pursued him, had she not spied four hazel eyes glaring at her from the doorway of his chambers. She retreated, instead, to her own rooms, where she sidled into a corner and cried.

After a while, she felt two hands gently ease the burden of her crown. Through falling tears, she saw her servant Chanah set aside the tiara. She asked the maid also to brush out her hair, and, while the girl stroked, Yod mused that Chanah would soon have two heads to tend.

— Are you expecting, ma'am?

— Expecting to be left for the bursar's daughters.

— You needn't worry about that.

— Why not? How would you know?

— I'm their elder sister.

— But you're a chambermaid, Chanah.

— What else was there for me to do, ma'am? I was His Majesty's mistress before he met you. Most of the palace servant girls were, child courtiers wooed and deserted, mocked publicly: a shame on their noble families. Father already acts as if the twins aren't his daughters. He'll disown them when your husband gets sick of them, and then they'll be scrubbing floors.

— Did you love the prince?

— Forgive me, ma'am. I still do.

Yod stared at Chanah. The glint of wet sapphire made the girl shudder. The princess embraced her. Then, in a soft voice, she vowed not to cry anymore, no matter what His Majesty did to her. She quietly declared that she'd no right to pity herself, with so many others so much more deserving of sympathy. And she silently reflected that they'd lost more, those poor servant girls, than she'd ever had—quickened mud less human than the coarsest criminal—while, to their disgrace, she'd been made a royal.

As Chanah retired to the servants' quarters, she left Yod with a feeling unfamiliar to her, neither pain nor pleasure, nor the mixed offspring of their union, the emotional siblings hatred and love. Rather, it was like an orphan taken in, adopted. She didn't know its name, but others called it compassion.

Raisa grew pregnant. Raina didn't. Each day, they had less in common than they'd had the day before. They started to bicker, intimately in the beginning, and, as the abyss widened, at a higher pitch. The whole palace heard their screeching. Each girl accused the other of trying to hoard all of His Majesty's attention when, truth be told, he no longer cared for either of them.

The prince was courting a new girl. Because she was his first cousin, he took the trouble to make the seduction clandestine. Only after he'd bedded her—a skittish little redhead foxed with freckles—did he dispense with subtlety, seating her on his lap at supper, and evicting the twins from his chambers.

The girls sought out their father. Squinting nearsightedly at the mismatched pair, he no longer recognized them as his daughters, and said, in case they were seeking employment, that he already had adequate servants. They went to their friends, girls their age with whom they'd both played before they'd become adult entertainment, but those young ladies were busy assembling trousseaus, and had already been given suitable maids of their own. Raisa and Raina scoured the palace for a touch of kindness, groveling at every door.

Of course none of this reached the princess, isolated in her chambers, until she asked Chanah what had happened to the twins since her husband had replaced them with his cousin.

— They got their comeuppance, ma'am, just as I promised.

— Their father won't have them back? He must have seen Raisa's condition.

— They can't even empty folks' bedpans, they're so besmirched. Give them another week, and they'll be begging in the street.

— I'll take them in.

— What do you mean?

— You're their sister. Go to them and say that they'll serve me.

The following morning, the twins stood in front of the princess, heads bowed, hands clenched. After just a week of living outdoors in the palace garden, they were as filthy as any forest urchin. Their silk gowns were stained from midnight raids on His Majesty's blackberry patch, ripped where the brambles had clawed back. Their pale skin was soiled from sleeping in flower beds. Their blond hair was matted with fern, and tangled together where their heads met as they huddled close for warmth at night. Shoulder to shoulder in front of the princess, they were inseparable, and what bound them more even than the knots in their hair was their shared fear.

Yod commanded them to look at her. They raised their hazel eyes. They took a deep breath. While she was dressed as simply as a farm girl—barefoot in a muslin frock, a braid of her own hair swept around her brow as a tiara—they saw that her poise, so recently toppled by them in the prince's chambers, had since risen higher than the palace towers.

They asked what she intended to do to them. She proposed that they bathe, offering her own tub, and that they rest, offering her own bed. She smiled at them, and left.

As the bath warmed their blood, the twins began to squabble again. Raina said that if Raisa hadn't gotten herself pregnant, the prince would still want them, to which Raisa responded that he would if only Raina weren't barren. Since birth, they'd been doted on as a pair. Each was only half herself; duality was their identity. Now one of them had grown distinct from the other, broken their biological mirror, and lucklessly lost them their prince, their father, every friend they'd ever had. Who'd betrayed whom? Raisa saw the difference in Raina, Raina saw the difference in Raisa, and, the longer they looked, the less each felt like herself.

Raisa grabbed Raina by the neck. Raina held Raisa's head underwater. Raisa's grasp slackened as she drowned. At the last moment, Raina released her, and Raisa came up for air, where she saw the princess standing above, watching over them both.

Her Majesty was no longer draped in mere muslin, but wore a vestment of red so vivid that it seemed to breathe. When she knelt, they saw that her robe was in fact alive: a conclave of cardinals nestled together, huddled around her. She reached out a gloved hand to them. Gently, she touched each girl on the cheek.

— Neither of you is to blame. *He's* the one who changed.

— But what if . . .

— Hush. This is his way. It's his misfortune. I was once like him. I know how it is not to feel.

— We brought him such pleasure.

— It empties right through him. The prince has no stomach for love, and passion without the capacity for devotion is appetite without the capacity for digestion.

The princess rose to her feet, shimmering in her robe as the birds shuffled their wings. She excused herself, as that evening she had to attend her husband's banquet honoring a foreign envoy. As she reached the door, the twins asked her how she could remain faithful to a man who'd jilted her.

— I'm not faithful to the prince. I feel for him, and I'm faithful to my emotion.

Over the next several years, Yod took in a dozen more of her husband's spent lovers. The prince scornfully referred to his wife's ever-more-crowded quarters as her harem, but, to those who deigned visit, her chambers looked more like an almshouse. With her personal allowance—the paltry sum annually disbursed from the royal coffers so that his majesty could keep his affairs separate from hers—she fed and clothed the girls. She also found them day jobs around the palace, while at night she taught them all that she'd learned about the world by living with demons. They were devoted to her, the girls, and, when they slept with her, shared pleasures that did not lapse with the hours.

Yet no matter how intimate they were with Yod, none of the girls could discern where she'd come from. Had she been the demons' queen before the prince tied her in wedlock? Did her royal line descend from a celestial throne, to which she'd eventually be restored, with them in angelic attendance? Since she never gave them the least little hint—she was as captive to her enigma amid servants as she'd been with the prince—they played guessing games while she was out at palace functions.

They could not, after all, accompany her to banquets and balls. At public processions, however, taking their place among commoners, they watched her, standing beside the prince in His Majesty's open coach. They watched, and what they'd seen as Yod's pathetic submission while they'd been his lovers, they now perceived as preternatural forbearance.

The grandest procession each year took place on the summer solstice, for His Majesty could not bear to be outshone by the sun. His guards roused the populace in darkness, and told them the route His Majesty's procession would take, so that wherever the prince looked on his long ride through city streets and over country roads, he'd see adoring subjects. Because he viewed folks in aggregate rather than recognizing their individuality, he never noticed that, Potemkin villagers, they were creeping along with his carriage.

His Majesty rose with the dawn. Leaving his mistress to sleep in, he went to his princess. She'd been up for many hours. Dark shadows of night lingered under her sapphire eyes. He didn't look her in the face, but only observed that the gown he'd called for made her appear even more supernal than he'd hoped: Yod wore nothing but doves.

The procession commenced, led by sentries polished in brass. Next in line were the nobles, mounted on horses, each bearing a coat of arms wrought in bronze, followed by courtiers carrying a fanfare on horn. Along the roadside, folks knelt. The royal carriage passed.

Now it happened that a foreigner, a traveling scholar, had the previous evening taken lodging for himself and his nag at a hostel along the procession route. He'd said that he'd come searching for a golem. The proprietor had answered that enchanted beings were forbidden in this country—the prince shared his power with nobody—but because the foreigner looked so weary, the hostel keeper had insisted that the poor man spend the night.

The scholar slept past dawn, nearly to noon, roused only by the rising cacophony outside. He unlatched his shutters, and saw hundreds of peasants scrambling from all directions toward the road below. He crawled under his bed in terror. He heard the crowd grow larger and louder, and then the sounding of a fanfare. Down on his knees, he crept back to the window. Like him, all the peasants were kneeling, as a dozen men, blowing brazen horns, passed on horseback, heralding their sovereign.

As the royal carriage turned the bend, the scholar's gaze fell on the princess. Three white doves crowned her head, her hair braided into a dark umber nest. The rest of the covey wove their wings around her body, breasts pressed to her tawny flesh. Each bird was ennobled with one of her gems, clasping in its beak an emerald or amethyst or, for her tiara, a star sapphire. Merely to be visible beside her, the prince had donned a full set of golden armor, and even then he looked like her lowly squire.

The coach rolled by the hostel. Her regal gaze glossed over the scholar. He winced. He called out to her. His cry joined the roadside chorus of peasants serenading their princess. He lost track of his words. The louder he shouted, the less certain he was even of which voice was his. Who knows what he said?

Who can say if Yod heard? Who knows if it was the crush of noise or the noonday heat that made the princess swoon and, in a flutter of doves, fall senseless on the street?

Not until the following evening was Meir admitted to the palace, and even then he was received only because he'd been mistaken, from his harsh accent and demanding manner, for an itinerant doctor. He was ushered into Her Majesty's chambers, where the prince knelt unattended, lips pressed to Yod's feverish forehead.

Hearing footsteps, the prince bristled, and clambered to his feet. A councillor introduced Meir. His majesty commanded the medic to tell him what he could about the princess.

— She's a golem.

— Her illness is not a joking matter.

— I'm the one who made her, Your Majesty. I made her as my mistress. Then she got away. For three years, I've been searching the world . . .

— She's my princess, of royal blood.

— She's a lump of mud.

— This is slander.

— Will you return her if I can prove that she's a golem, sire?

— If you can't prove it, I'll have you hanged for slighting my beloved wife.

By then both were standing over her as she moaned in her sleep, beaded in sweat. Meir whispered that if the prince brushed back her hair, he'd find a mark on her forehead. At a table in the corner, the scholar drew the vital sign in red ink. He came back to Yod. The prince clutched her hair, and, with a yank, bared Her Majesty's scalp.

. . .

When Yod awoke late that night, shivering beneath sweat-drenched sheets, Raisa was there to comfort her. She fetched woolen blankets, heaped them on the bed. And, to amuse the princess, she described the peculiar man her husband had received while she was asleep, evidently a quack, who'd penned a strange figure on a slip of paper and then stood over her while the prince tore at her hair.

Yod blanched. She asked Raisa to bring her the drawing. For several minutes, they stared at it together. Then Yod swept back her tresses.

— Does it match?

— Does what match, Your Majesty?

— Does the symbol resemble the blemish on my forehead?

— Pardon me for saying so, but your forehead is spotless.

— Then he can't take me back.

— I don't understand.

— I don't either, Raisa. Tell me, did the stranger say anything to my husband, after they'd examined me?

— He was speechless. The prince called for his sentries. The execution is in the morning. Can nobody cure you, Princess?

Yod didn't respond. For a while, Raisa arranged blankets on the bed. Then she left Her Majesty to rest.

In Yod's dreams, Meir was put to death. As he fell from the gallows, noosed at the neck, she felt a sudden weightlessness, complete release from her past. In a snap, the sensation passed, overwhelmed by a burden that her frail human body couldn't carry, yet she could not drop.

Her eyes opened. Looking at the paper inscription in the dawn light, she understood that the mark on her forehead had faded away as it had lost meaning. She was no longer a golem. She could barely move a limb, so completely had strength succumbed to feeling.

Outside, Yod heard nails being driven into a wooden gallows. She bit her lip. She bit down so hard that it bled. She called for Raisa. Raina, who'd taken her place, hurried to her bed. The princess held the slip of paper in front of the girl, and ordered her to draw, as perfectly as she could, the insignia that she saw.

— Draw it where?

— On my forehead.

— With what?

— With my blood.

— Have you lost your mind?

— We'll soon know.

Shuddering, the girl touched a plump finger to Her Majesty's lip. She took a breath, and, in a single stroke, inscribed the inscrutable cipher on the princess's forehead.

Yod grasped her hand, and kissed it. Then she sent Raina away to watch the execution.

Raisa was feeding her young son when her twin sister reached her. Raina tried to describe the princess's strange behavior. She held out her finger, but neither could find any blood there.

— She didn't explain the drawing?

— She said to attend the hanging.

Together with Raisa's boy, the twins hustled to the gallows. Most of the palace was already assembled, as were many peasants. The foreigner stood on a platform. Stripped to a loincloth, hands tied behind his back, skinny legs quivering, he no longer looked so learned. He stared at the ground. Everywhere folks jeered, though none of them knew what crime had been committed.

His Majesty commanded quiet. He read the accusation: slander of the ailing princess. Would anyone speak in the guilty man's defense?

A single voice cleaved the silence. The crowd split, to let Yod pass.

The princess wore none of her regalia, merely a white bed-sheet, clutched around her trembling body with one hand while she groped her way forward with the other. At last she stood in front of her husband. Loud enough for all to hear, she declared that the accused had not slandered her.

— He called you a golem.

— I am one.

— You're delirious.

— I'm a golem, sire, and I was made by that man.

— You're sick.

— He made me his mistress. You could learn a few tricks from him.

— You're mad.

— You won't believe me. See my forehead.

Yod threw back her umber hair. The prince stared at the blood mark. His face flushed red. With a fist, he wiped out the blotch.

Her trembling stopped. Her body dropped to his feet. He knelt to lift her. Meir broke free of his ropes.

The prince tore away her sheet. The scholar sought her heart. Meir shook his head. There was no beat. In the shadow of the gallows, both men held her together, and began to weep.

As their tears touched her, Yod flowed away, a river of mud between their fingers.

YOD-ALEF THE MURDERER

Wise men say that you can never truly be lost: Death will find you in the end. Forgive their misinformation, for they've never been to the distant city, rarely remembered by intrepid traders, once forgotten by the grim reaper.

Of course, folks who lived there didn't notice at first. It was a big enough place that nobody cared about the fate of others, and those of an age to consider mortality, to expect the end, simply assumed that death was on another street, or just around the corner. Only the grave diggers complained, and there wasn't much sympathy for men whose money was made on misfortune.

In fact, a whole winter passed before respectable people began to comment on the phenomenon. They asked one another why there were no longer any casket processions, whether funerals had gone out of fashion. They tried to recollect the last time that an acquaintance had died. Perhaps the grave diggers weren't such grifters after all; maybe they'd pawned their picks and had to cadge their meals for a reason. Everybody knew how difficult the city was to reach on horseback. Was it possible that death, additionally burdened by cloak and scythe, had given up the shlep?

Beyond death's ken: Never in their lives had folks felt so lucky. A feverish giddiness spread through the city as swiftly as an epidemic. The heat of invincibility drove people, delirious, into the streets, where they danced with neighbors who had been strangers the previous day. And that night more children were conceived than there were branches on the tree of life.

In the following month, old feuds were resolved, families reunited, friendships renewed. People became familiar with everyone in their neighborhood. Given immortality, folks could afford to be generous on a daily basis. Or, rather, in eternal terms, a slight costs more than kindness, a grudge more than forgiveness. With forever on the horizon, life's entire perspective shifted.

Yet people also noticed less felicitous changes. Tradesmen seldom did their work, reckoning, not unreasonably, that they could always get to it later. As a result, shopkeepers carried less, and kept holiday hours. Which left laborers with so little to purchase with their wages that they couldn't be bothered to lift a finger.

Economies collapsed. When they realized that their masters would never retire, apprentices burned their indentures. And the absence of inheritance effectively ended the trade in burghers' sons and daughters, the merger of bloodlines, the birth of dynasties. Divested of death, the city edged into rigor mortis.

The only ones who weren't idle then were the academicians. These twelve learned men, whose role ordinarily was to ensure the city's place in history, had been asked by the governor to apply their scholarship to the future. The most senior of the savants, the renowned alchemist-astrologer Akiva Alter, accepted the brief on behalf of the cabal, assuming absolute authority over life-and-death matters.

For one month, they researched the future in sealed chambers. Each man wore a beard the length of his tenure, and a gown and cap colored according to his discipline: black for classics, white for logic, red for anatomy, purple for divinity. Akiva Alter presided, richly robed in silver and gold, his beard rolled out like an ancient manuscript from the head of the table to the foot. He wanted to know whether, in all human history, the angel of death had ever failed to appear at the end of a life span. Benesh the necromancer reported that, excepting for beings not falling under death's jurisdiction, such as dybbuks and golems, nobody survived indefinitely. Which naturally provoked the question: Had the city fallen out of time? Iyov the geographer could find no evidence for so titanic a tectonic shift, and Pinchas the anatomist could vouch that people continued to age, to which the mathematician Menache added that there were new children, droves of them, born every day.

Now it doesn't take a savant to know that a city can hold only as many people as there are names—just as the sky can hold only as many stars as there are numbers—and to see the horrific effects of perpetual aging, one has only to look at the wrinkled crust of the wretched earth. In a thousand years, the city would be mountainous with living flesh, bodies no longer individually sentient, a roiling sediment of collective agony, dumb to all but the mercilessly enduring present. While there was some dispute among the savants as to whether this human mountain would be domed or peaked, and whether it would be barren or forested with evergreens, the academicians could all agree that such concerns were academic. A practical solution was wanted. Following one week's fast with neither talk nor sleep, Akiva Alter sat down, rolled out his beard, and proposed one: an idea so ingenious that it was adopted without discussion.

. . .

Like everyone else, Yod-Alef the bricklayer and his wife, Sisel, were summoned several days later to the great assembly hall, where they stood in line for hours, waiting to draw lots. Ordinarily the loss of a day would have angered Yodal (as everyone called him), for he took his work very seriously. He could mortar and set from dawn to dusk without rest, laying twice the thousand-brick standard of his trade. It was for this competency, this diligence, that Sisel several years before had married Yodal instead of one of the richer bricklayers who'd courted her, such as tall, handsome Hebel, former apprentice to her dead father. But lately it made no difference how many bricks her husband could handle, since nobody bothered to build. This was the first time Yodal had had a place to be in ages. He saw his fellow tradesmen and friends, and all of them agreed that lining up was a fine idea: A line had a start and a finish, a direction, a purpose—even if nobody could explain it, or reckon what the lottery was about.

Yodal's turn came at last, after Sisel had drawn. Watched over by twelve ancient men in colored gowns, he reached his hand into a box the size of a coffin, and closed his fist around a little wooden ball. He looked at it. Sisel's had been white. His was black.

The academicians conferred in a strange tongue. They gathered around Yodal. The eldest, robed in silver and gold, laid his hands on the bricklayer's shoulders, and commanded him to follow them. As he walked, Yodal heard Sisel begin to cry. He glanced back. He saw Hebel reaching his arms around her slender figure, to comfort her.

There was no supper for Yodal when he came home, past midnight. Sisel sat in front of the dark fireplace, a cauldron in her lap, into which her tears dropped.

— What happened to Hebel?

— Who cares, Yodal? All this time, I've been waiting here for you.

She told him that she'd had no idea if he'd ever return, and made him promise not to abandon her again. His vows swelled into kisses, and then a deeper cleaving as they carried each other to bed.

In the morning, Sisel wanted her husband to tell her where he'd been with those odd men. She gazed at his reflection in her looking glass as she asked, brushing her fine red hair. He was not handsome at all, the man she'd married, built thick like a stump, yet that only fiercened her ardor: With her moist eyes and tight waist, she was attractive to every man—a reflexive passion—whereas she had chosen specifically to desire him. Sisel was a willful girl who knew how to have her way. She sat by her husband and stroked his head.

— It can't be that bad. And our vows are mutual, Yodal. No matter what, I'll be here for you.

— It isn't good.

— Do they want you to love a girl besides me?

— They've . . . they've appointed me . . . grim-reaper-by-proxy. Until further notice, I'm supposed to be the angel of death.

Sisel's hand pulled away, and only with the greatest effort did she bring it again to where it had been. She swallowed a tremor in her throat.

— They can do that?

— They've never tried it before. They're not sure, but they say it's the only chance we've got.

From the pocket of his coat, he withdrew a warrant, and unfurled it on the bed. A scourge of black lettering raged across a whole sheepskin of vellum, branded with the governor's red wax bull. Neither Yodal nor his wife could read it, but both agreed that it was a terrible document.

— What do you do with it?

— I carry it when I tell folks that their time has come.

— Then what?

— I think they're supposed to pass away.

— I liked it better when you were a bricklayer.

Still, Sisel adored her husband, and was anxious to aid him in his work. Since death was a job to be done at night, that meant preparing him a good early supper, waiting up while he did his rounds, and warming him with a bowl of soup when he came home. Not that the change in trade was as simple as altered eating habits. In fact, grim-reaping had very little in common with bricklaying, and even if he'd been asked to build schooners with his hod and trowel, poor Yodal would have been less at sea.

The academicians weren't helpful. While they were meticulous about the grim business of who he had to visit, backing the latest astrological data with breakthroughs in necromancy and divination, they gave no consideration to how the actual reaping ought to be done.

On his first night, Yodal was sent to see an old burgher named Meyer, who lived alone with his servant in a mansion on a hill. The burgher received Yodal at bedside. In a voice that crackled like falling snow, he asked the tradesman to take the chair nearest his head. Yodal sat, and, opening his warrant, tried to figure out where to begin. He gazed at Meyer. The man's skin was so pale, and stretched so tightly over his skull, that, for a wishful moment, the reaper-by-proxy thought his grisly job done. Then Meyer peeled back his lips. He said that, from the warrant, he understood what Yodal wanted, but that he wasn't ready yet. Accustomed to delinquent accounts, the bricklayer asked him how long he needed.

— I was expecting to live forever. Come back later.

— Tomorrow night?

— In a while, Yodal. There must be others who can go before.

When Yodal got home, Sisel took care to embrace him as if he were an ordinary tradesman. She gave him some potato soup, salted with tears. After a silence, she asked him about his work.

— I was a failure.

— Does that mean you don't have to be grim reaper any-more?

— You don't like my job.

— I want you to be happy, Yodal. But if we have children, think what it will be like for them.

In bed, they tried again to make her pregnant, as they had every night since their wedding. After a while, she forgot what her husband did for a living. And the two were drawn together anew.

A rumor awakened the city the following morning. First the servants heard it. Soon it rose from the houses where they worked, up through the echelons of wealth and power to the great assembly hall, where every bell tolled in the tower.

Then it was true: Someone was dead. Meyer the burgher had died in the night. But—here folks spoke in a whisper—it wasn't on account of the grim reaper. Meyer had been finished off by Yodal the bricklayer. A murderer? By warrant of the governor!

In another time and place, there might have been protests, riots, gunfire: Shoot the messenger. However, everybody in the city had lived long enough without the angel of death to want someone else extinguished—universal immortality being less agreeable even than equal distribution of wealth—and Yodal was as good as anyone to play grand macabre.

He was the last to know what had happened. He slept through rumors and bells until noon, when Sisel woke him and repeated everything that people were saying in the market-place.

— You told me that you didn't do it.

— I didn't. Meyer asked me to come back.

— No need for that. He'll be buried by the time you slaughter your next victim.

Yodal didn't know whether to be proud or distraught. Overnight he lost all his friends: Everyone knew what he did, and avoided him like the plague. Only Sisel stayed with him, enduring the social quarantine, resolutely redoubling her devotion. She stirred up ever more elaborate soups, and threw ever more effort into giving him children. She missed him awfully during the hours he was gone, and throbbed with jealousy when his appointment was with a woman. But naturally Yodal cared only for his Sisel, and did his work for her sake. Grim-reaping brought him a good salary—a government contract on which to raise a family—and wasn't nearly as labor-intensive as mortaring bricks for a living. In fact, with his warrant and reputation, he needed merely to make an appearance to have his effect.

Certainly, folks tried to negotiate. While all could agree that life in the city was much improved by the return of death, understandably everyone wanted to enjoy the benefits. Yodal was always courteous and empathetic, generous with his condolences. He offered to return the following night when requested, but there was never any need: By morning, the man or woman would be dead.

Occasionally there were accidents—folks frightened to death when they saw him pass under a streetlight—or complications of other kinds. A pawnbroker offered him a wealth of diamonds for a six-month furlough. A young trader proposed a partnership in his business to spare him and take his father instead. A young woman approached him at home, promising her body if only he'd murder her husband.

Scrupulous Yodal refused all of it, patiently explaining that he didn't decide who died, that it was reckoned by academicians on arcane charts in secret chambers. (The accidents they wrote off as accounting errors.) Yodal was just the deliveryman, and had no more say about a life span than a farmer did over the turn of seasons.

Still, some didn't believe him. One man attacked him, and had a stroke. One woman ran away, only to be knocked flat in the street by a horse and buggy. The only person who nearly lived to see daylight was the philosopher Meshulam, who held Yodal for hours in contemplation.

The philosopher received Yodal in his study, where he poured some fine brandy, and posed more questions than the bricklayer had asked in a lifetime. Yodal didn't understand any of them—though they extended from the inner realm of ethics to the outer reaches of cosmology—and he never knew whether to nod yes or no. But Meshulam scarcely noticed him. The old man had as little interest in answers as he had in bricks: Answers confined questions. So the philosopher always asked more. He might have gone on forever, were it not for the liquor. Meshulam grew drowsy. Yodal slipped away.

The soup was cold when the bricklayer got home. His wife was in bed. Her pillow was bruised. Her eyes were shut with hurt.

— You're out later every night. You love your job more than you love me.

— I tried to get away. The philosopher Meshulam had some questions.

— If it isn't your job that you love, then you must have a mistress. Come here. I can smell the liquor.

Yodal obeyed her. She pulled him close. As they made love, she begged him never to leave her again.

The following evening, Yodal told Akiva Alter that he wished to retire. He'd brought death to nearly a hundred people, sometimes half a dozen in a night, he pointed out. He'd worked hard and done his job well, but his real trade was bricklaying, and he'd heard from Hebel that business was improving.

He missed his work. He missed the daylight. The wise man was understanding. A replacement might be found, the next night, even. But first the day's chosen had to be culled. The grim-reaper-by-proxy asked for the death roll. Akiva Alter gave him only one name: Sisel.

— That can't be. Sisel is my wife.

— Her time has come.

— She's healthy and young.

— You've killed off children.

— That was different. I live for Sisel.

— You know how this works, Yodal. Our charts are infallible.

— Let me see them.

— You're an ignorant tradesman.

Still, Akiva Alter led the bricklayer up into the locked observatory, the tallest building in the city, where the charts were kept.

For all his experience with plumb bob and line pins, Yodal was astonished by the complex machines stored there. He gaped at an enormous clockwork of brass gears and steel springs, the sole purpose of which, Akiva Alter showed him, was to roll up his beard. Then he showed Yodal mysterious spools of numbers that he said represented the most advanced research on the planet, calibrated to the equinoxes, verified in consultation with sun and moon. Yodal couldn't remember any of the fancy cosmological questions posed by Meshulam with which to confound Akiva Alter, so he simply asked the academician:

— What if the stars are wrong?

— Look at them. They map all time. In the whole span of history, they've never changed their position.

The bricklayer looked up through the observatory's oculus, in the direction that the seated savant was pointing his jeweled finger, and watched, an instant later, a streak of light arc the distance of darkness.

From that moment, the cosmos was different for Yodal. Nothing was fixed. As he spiraled down the staircase, he scarcely heard Akiva Alter calling after him about necromancy and divination and the infallibility of learned science. Sisel would live. That was the only certainty. Yodal would not bring death to her. He wouldn't visit her with that. He'd never see her again, but what was his happiness measured against her life? Like the comet, he vanished into the blackness of night.

For many years, Yod-Alef wandered the continent, working for bricklayers and stonemasons as a laborer, never staying anywhere more than a season, nor giving away his real name, lest his Sisel chance to hear it spoken, and pursue him. He claimed to have no wife, which often encouraged young widows to court him. But his solitary love for Sisel was inviolable, absolute, and girls' well-meaning efforts to cleave it pained him like a brick ax to the heart. In her absence, Sisel occupied him through day and night. Because he could tell the truth about himself to no one, she was, as he remembered her, his sole companion.

Yodal's fellow laborers didn't know what to make of him. They wondered how a man his age could have no good stories, how it was possible that nothing the least bit interesting had ever happened to him. But he didn't drink with them, or share their whores, so, following a few sarcastic comments, they generally forgot about him, and, by the end of the season, he was able to slip away without anyone remembering that he'd been there, let alone caring where he'd gone.

Towns are people divided by walls: Yodal could have run away every month, every week, each hour of every day, and have still found places in want of his anonymous skills. He was suited to the itinerant life. Bricks and mortar were his freedom.

One morning, he got into a conversation with another laborer about towns where they'd worked. The man called himself Motke, and, while he was young enough to be Yodal's son, they'd many similarities. In the first place, Motke was unusually handy for a common laborer, adept with line pins and plumb bob, so proficient with square and bevel that the master's apprentice had several times begrudgingly taken instruction from him. In the second place, he was exceedingly discreet, which alternately gave the impression that he had nothing to say and that he was in possession of unspeakable secrets. And in the third place, he was built thick and strong like Yodal, which was why both had been hired for the hard work of lifting bricks three stories to set a spire atop the town hall.

As they spoke, Yodal recognized the dialect peculiar to his native city, the patois of an isolated place with many terms for immediate proximity and few for long distance. Motke was the first person he'd met from his region since leaving, the first man who might know if his Sisel was well. Yet naturally he couldn't say her name. Instead, he simply asked about the city. Motke looked him over with care. At last he bent near and said:

— You're from there, too?

— I had a job in the city a long time ago.

— Which master did you work for?

— A fellow called . . . Hebel.

— Hebel was my father.

— He wasn't married when I was there. Who's your mother?

— Her name is Sisel. Do you know her?

— I suppose that I don't.

The master called Yodal to fetch more lime for mortar. Motke watched him sling the wooden hod across his shoulder and head toward the quarry.

Several days later, the hod was seen in pieces at the bottom of a cliff. A search for Yodal's body followed. Not even his bones could be found.

The widow Sisel was living in a tiny hovel built of rough granite in the hills above the city. Brick and mortar had brought her nothing but despair: the loss of one husband after another, and then her only son. She was still marriageable—her beauty had aged with the firm resolve of fine marble—but what good had men ever been? When the matchmakers came, she slammed the door on them. Nor did she go out much anymore. Her childhood friendships hadn't survived her marriage to Yodal, and Hebel's companions had been rough-hewn masons who wanted only to lay her.

And, in any case, so many people had died. Ancient Akiva Alter had been the first after Yodal's departure, found the following morning in his observatory, expired over the celestial tables, one jeweled finger pointed stiffly toward an empty sky. Within weeks, the other eleven academicians were deceased. Nobody thought to replace them, nor to appoint a new grim-reaper-by-proxy. Folks reckoned that death had finally recalled the way to their distant city, and repaid Yodal's makeshift undertaking by making him angel's apprentice. Only Sisel was dissatisfied with that explanation for her husband's sudden disappearance. She believed that he'd bartered death for life with another girl, younger and prettier than she. She confided this in Hebel, who naturally encouraged such faithless suspicions. He courted her openly. Nobody was surprised to see that, within a year, they were married and a son was born.

As a husband, Hebel showed neither competency nor diligence. His work kept him away from home all day long, and at night his many mistresses occupied him. He tolerated Motke on the job—the boy was free labor after all, capable of mixing mortar and tying down scaffold—but Sisel he ignored when he wasn't teaching the kid a lesson by banging her like a board.

Shortly after Motke's twelfth birthday, Hebel was crushed under a mislaid pile of bricks. That effectively ended the boy's apprenticeship. He went to find work in other cities. Five years lapsed, and then five more. Sisel waited for him, a little sadder and poorer each season, expectant at every knock that he'd come back—only to be faced with another meddlesome matchmaker.

The knocking stopped for a time, and then returned in the third month of her eleventh year alone. She unhitched the latch.

Yod-Alef stood in front of her. Sisel dropped to her knees, instantly repenting everything she'd ever said and done: He burned with such fury that she imagined he actually had been taken in by the angel of death, and, apprenticeship served, became damnation itself. Then she saw that Yodal had aged, which, as she knew, supernatural creatures don't do, at least in human ways. She stood up. She held out her hand.

He didn't move. He tried to speak, but his heat was too great. The words simmered over in sobs, and Sisel had to pull him across the doorstep by clasping his wrist. She sat him down. She stroked his hair as she had years before.

He bristled. He stared at her.

— How could you do this to me, Sisel? How could you marry Hebel? How could you have a son?

— You abandoned me. You ran off with another girl.

— Is that what Hebel told you?

— Isn't it true?

Of course it wasn't, though poor Yodal, who'd scarcely spoken in two decades, had a very hard time persuading her: Even after he'd told her every detail about his life, from Akiva Alter and the comet to Motke and the broken hod, she refused for hours to believe that Hebel had had so many mistresses while

Yodal had had none. But even jealous Sisel could hold on to her delusion for only so long. Yodal's love for her had made him leave her, and what had she gone and done?

— No, no, Yodal. I hated you for what you did, but I married Hebel for your sake.

— You might as well have slit my throat.

— I was pregnant when you left me. I couldn't raise Motke alone. He was all I had left of you. Yodal, Motke is your son.

— Does he know?

— I told him when Hebel died. That's why he went away. For the past eleven years and three months, he's been searching for you.

Both parents wanted him back then, but who could say where he'd gone in the week since Yodal abandoned him to avenge Sisel's infidelity by fulfilling Akiva Alter's prophecy? His warrant had no expiration date. He'd come to implement it, and now he couldn't rescind it. He couldn't leave Sisel, even for a moment, without taking her life away. He couldn't run off to fetch Motke, and even for them to travel together was too risky: A misstep could separate the lovers, young again to each other, for an eternity.

So they stayed. Yodal hitched the latch on her door. Sisel brought him to bed. In their embrace, they encompassed their world.

Half a century passed. Motke traveled to every country, other continents even, searching for his father. In all those years, only one man had moved him to believe that Yod-Alef could be found. But then that man had dropped his hod from a cliff and vanished. And now that he was too old to labor, Motke was walking home.

In his native city, he no longer knew anybody. New buildings, more imposing, had replaced old ones. None of his brickwork remained. He asked old folks what had happened to his mother. Only one man recognized Sisel's name, and said—he had to smile—that she lived with her husband in a stone hovel from which they hadn't emerged in decades. He pointed to the hill. He described the trail.

Motke was a sensible man. He didn't believe the codger any more than he'd trusted those fables, popular when he was a child, about the grim reaper losing his way to the city. Motke was sensible, but he also needed a place to stay. He followed the trail. He climbed the hill. He knocked at the door of the stone hovel.

For a while, nobody answered. Then he heard a single pair of feet shuffle across the floor. The latch rattled and fell. The door opened. Motke looked into the blind eyes of the oldest creature he'd ever seen.

At first he guessed it was a woman. Next he figured it was a man. Then he perceived, from the serene expression, that it was both his mother and his father, so many years together, so close to each other, that they had cleaved into one being.

YOD-BEIT THE REBEL

Ousted from the heavens for crimes against paradise, angels burn bright as they fall through the night. Folks call them shooting stars, and even wish on them, but no one believes the euphemism: Wish what they will, folks can only hope that those shamed angels incinerate in the descent, for a seraph that endures the plummet will bedevil humanity forever.

One morning after a terrible celestial downpour, a crippled little girl shambled from town to town, begging for a place to rest. She was as pale as fright and as slight as chance. Evidently she'd been a victim of the nocturnal mayhem—bloody and broken as if ravaged by demons—and if anyone asked what had happened, she bowed her head, shrouding her face behind hair of tarnished silver, and started sobbing.

She didn't answer when folks inquired who her parents were or where she'd come from. In each village, the story was the same: Questions hardened into suspicions, and, when the girl couldn't even say her name, sharpened into accusations. These were dangerous times, the villagers informed her, peering through her veil of hair into blue eyes washed pale with tears. How could they be sure that she wasn't herself a beast?

She opened her mouth. They pointed at her teeth, small and serrated. She was the devil, they decreed, and if heaven didn't want her, they sure as hell didn't either. Too stunned to protest, she was chased out of each village, pelted with dirt and cursed as a monster, the cause of man's anguish on earth.

She'd begun to wonder whether what folks told her was true, when she wandered into a village quite unlike the others. The town had no walls, but was built on a swamp. Nor were there buildings of brick and stone as she'd seen elsewhere, merely dirt huts. Sunk to her knees in muck, she knocked on the first door she reached. Silence. She looked around. Not a soul to be seen, though it was past noon. She pushed the door open. Into the darkness, she plunged.

The muck was much thicker inside, a soft bed beneath her aching body. She curled up. She slept. She dreamed that she was home again. All was immaculate, a land unsoiled: a life of gilt and polished marble. The air was fragrance on a breeze of music. She tried to inhale—and could not breathe. All at once awake, she found herself under a crush of rancid flesh.

With her lungs' last draft, she screamed. Pressing closer, her captors urged her to hush. They asked, with a trace of offense, *Yod-Beit, don't you recognize us?*

She opened her eyes wide. She had not heard her name in many days. The last time, *Yod-Beit* had been uttered as a curse. If she'd lamented never to hear it again, this was worse.

— Are you demons?

— We don't say that here. I'm your cousin Boaz. These are your cousins Hudes and Pinchas.

Try as she might, Yod-Beit could not see the family resemblance. Of course every seraph had heard rumors about what happened to outcast angels, the monstrosities they became in the shadow of heaven, but even death was more fathomable to Yod-Beit than so terrible a fate. She ran trembling fingers across her face.

— Do I look like you now?

— Only a few broken bones, some bruises. It's miraculous.

— But my skin isn't . . . My nose and ears haven't . . .

— It makes no difference, Yod-Beit. You're one of us.

For several months, they nursed Yod-Beit to health. Pinchas dressed her wounds. Hudes fed her soups. And Boaz talked to her through the blackest hours of night.

He told her about the cruelties of humans. In heaven, she'd been taught, like all young seraphim, that humans were good yet easily misled, and, while her education had been abbreviated by her fall, Yod-Beit tenaciously held on to this wisdom, her only celestial souvenir, and repeated it often. Boaz was patient with her—she'd never had to reason before—but persistent.

— What do angels know of human nature? They've never lived here.

— In our classes they said . . .

— When you were neediest, were people kind to you?

— They thought I might be a demon, and dangerous. Why do you torment them?

— Since the beginning of time, they've shunned us. They're more heartless than the angels above. They've pushed us into the swamps and raised their town walls, just because they don't like the looks of us.

Yod-Beit had to confess, if only to herself, that the looks of the demons she'd met didn't appeal to her either. On the other hand, no angel in heaven, as pretty as they were, had ever cared for her as these coarse devils did.

Even demons she hadn't known in heaven would come to visit her, bearing delicacies that couldn't possibly have come from the swamps, sweets that would sparkle on the palate of a princess. They also brought her luxuries, silks and satins unfit for their bloated bodies, that complimented her fine figure like a courtly suitor. And while she modeled that lacy clothing, nibbling on those dainty morsels, her new companions told their stories.

They'd strayed for decades following their fall, some of them, shuttered from civilization, without finding others in their condition. They'd been chased by peasants, taunted by children, jumped by vagabonds. Dogs and vultures had fed on their festering flesh while they slept. The stories never ended before Yod-Beit began to sob.

Crying still bewildered her. In heaven, there'd been no bodily fluids. Emotions never spilled. The only water was in reflecting pools, perfectly calm, eternally still. Her tears embarrassed her. She tried to constrain them as fitfully, to conceal them as falteringly, as a first menstruation. She lowered her face behind tarnished silver hair. But, unlike those humans who'd questioned what her upset hid, her fellow demons responded to what it revealed. Sympathetic to her sympathy, they steeped her tears in chamomile, and serenaded her to sleep.

The demons coddled Yod-Beit. She was their pet. They called her Beitzel. Only Boaz was worried that she might be spoiled. In her dreams, she sometimes still murmured those empty homilies about humanity that were taught in heaven. To be so naïve in this world of evil was a danger to her, a threat to them all. Boaz gathered his brethren. The time had come to teach Yod-Beit a lesson.

They invited her on a midnight picnic. The urge to get out of the swamp, if only for an evening, overwhelmed even the embarrassment she felt to be seen in their unsightly company. She dressed in her finest lace—scant trace of white thread against pale flesh—clenching it at the waist as they slopped through the mud to firm ground.

Boaz led them to an orchard. At one end was a stretch of grass, where the demons urged Beitzel to rest while they gathered apples. She settled down in the field, not unpleased to see them leave. Caressed by moonlight, she shut her eyes. She listened to the winds. There was no music in them, but she could hear voices, deep and melodious. Looking up, she found two tall woodsmen.

They asked her name. *Beitzel,* she said softly, and smiled.

— We've never met a girl called Beitzel. You're not from around here.

— Not really, no.

— Are you alone?

— You're with me now.

— Would you like to come with us?

She gazed at them, and imagined heaven. She nodded. They lifted her to her feet and drew her into the orchard.

Their grasp tightened in the shadows. She could no longer see their faces. They pressed her against a tree. One gripped her neck while the other tore away her lace. A knee drove her legs apart. A hand reached up her crotch, seeking something she never knew existed. She struggled to see what they wanted from her, stripped bare, but they had her upside down, and she couldn't speak through the pain as they tore at her seamless skin.

For several moments more, Boaz watched from a treetop. Then, at his call, the demons were upon them. While Hudes wrapped Beitzel in her arms, the others felled the woodsmen. Hudes urged her not to watch what came next, but Yod-Beit was too enthralled to feel horror. As the men began to bleed, she begged to get nearer. She didn't need more proof that people were evil, but how seductive she found it to see them ravaged on her behalf! The carnage at her feet delighted her more even than the lace that she'd lost. She dipped a finger in the slaughter and touched it to her tongue. The taste swelled through her like a first kiss.

Later that night, back in her bed, she secretly pressed the

same finger between her legs. She easily found what those men had been searching for, though she'd have sworn that nothing had been there before.

Yod-Beit never missed another ambush. The world was overrun with people. There was much justice to be done.

The demons found their work made easier by Beitzel. Previously they'd needed to hide until folks accidentally strayed, whereas Yod-Beit simply had to appear angelic, and men would be tempted to their fate by their own sinister plans.

Almost every night, she'd stroll through some woods or nap in a field, where folks would find her and, scarcely looking over their shoulder, try to have their way with her. Some wanted the wealth they reckoned she had, on account of her rich dress, but Yod-Beit was more interested in the men who sought her celestial flesh. Each had his own strut and his own smell. The demons never let them get far enough with her before the slaughter, though, for her to learn, quite, what a man could do to a girl.

Beitzel encouraged folks toward where the demons were least able to protect her. She eagerly risked injury. She bruised easily. Yet her body ached only where it wasn't touched.

Impressed by their cousin's daring, inspired by her dedication to the resistance, Boaz and his brethren were emboldened to escalate their rebellion against the human race. Pinchas proposed that they take a town.

— People would notice that. They'd have to respect us.

— Which village would we raid, though?

— Why not the small one across the forest? Aren't you sick of living in a swamp? Humans have wooden houses and flower gardens.

— They also have stone walls and iron gates to protect their villages at night.

That was a problem for the demons. Up in heaven, there'd been nowhere to climb: So strong in humans, the required muscles were undeveloped in angels, and down below the poor devils could scarcely overcome gravity to mount an apple tree. Too self-conscious to discuss this, they fell into silence. Only little Beitzel knew what to do.

— Let me go to their village in daylight. Then I can help you through the gates at night.

— You'll never be trusted, Beitzel.

— I'll need some time.

— Alone with them? You don't know the ways of men. You don't know how they can hurt you.

There was no dissuading Yod-Beit, though, and her previous accomplishments were unassailable. So they taught her all the human skills that they knew, how to cook and clean and knit and sew. They taught her customs, too, such as the way a girl curtsies when she's greeted, covers her mouth when she laughs, bows her head when she prays. She found all of these traditions funny, especially the last one: Did folks believe that heaven lay at their feet? She practiced holding her hand in front of her mouth as she giggled, and then, curtsying in a hempen frock that Hudes found for her, set out to become a normal girl.

Mendel the blacksmith spent most days sitting alone at a cold forge, wishing that he had a more worthy trade. His neighbor Lev the butcher worked from dawn to dusk, carving fresh meat. Folks regularly had to eat, but, once they'd bought an iron skillet, skillfully made, they wouldn't need another for decades. Occasionally people reminded Mendel that he'd wrought the town gates—as fine a tribute to his craft as any man could want—forgetting that the job had been done by his father, years before he was born: As short and slight as his father had been, Mendel felt only further shrunken by the dead man's enduring reputation.

One afternoon, while blowing dust from his bellows, Mendel observed a strange girl standing in the corner of his shop. He couldn't say whether she'd been there for a minute or all day, but she curtsied when he turned, and asked if perchance he'd a job for her.

— My furnace has been dark for weeks. There isn't even work for me.

— I could cook your meals and wash your clothes. I'm very capable.

— In this town nobody can afford a housekeeper, miss, least of all a blacksmith. You need to go to the city, where folks are all rich, and do nothing but feast.

— I can't. I'm afraid.

— Why?

— Demons. They had me as their slave. I barely escaped. You have to save me, Mister Smith.

Mendel scrutinized the girl with greater care than before. He knew that strangers weren't to be trusted, and he'd often been tricked by the fraudulent offers and counterfeit currencies of foreigners, yet, when she met his eyes, his whole shop glowed. He watched a tear drop, then another. Lest the light be extinguished, he vowed to protect her.

— I'll fetch Lev. He's very shrewd. He'll know what to do.

— Please, not yet. Keep me as your secret. When people ask, say that I was sent by a cousin. You never know who might be a demon.

Beitzel picked up a broom, and began to sweep. She swept the dirt to the back of the room, and then she swept it to the front. She repeated this feat for Mendel a dozen times, always with the utmost neatness, brushing the dirt back and forth without ever whisking a speck of it out the open door.

That didn't bother the blacksmith, who was enraptured

just to watch her delight in her own industriousness. Mendel reckoned that she'd been raised in a noble family, where she'd only seen maids sweep, a notion supported by her other peculiar behaviors. When Beitzel cleaned his clothes, for example, she was prone to forget the soap or water, and, mending them, she'd stitch several garments together in a way that might fit a griffin or a chimera, but not a regular four-limbed blacksmith. Oddest of all was her cooking. Filling a pot with whatever she could find, she'd heat it over a fire, and look flummoxed when the process didn't render edible her offering of bones or rocks or—God forbid—pig iron.

Failure battered her harder than the harshest husband. Spoiled meals roiled her to tears. And seeing Mendel amend her mending made her rend her own clothing. When Beitzel grew upset, he turned his back on the trouble she'd caused, and held her until her frustration was forgotten. Sometimes he'd catch her looking up at him as if she expected something else, and her breath on his neck would stoke a furnace he'd never before felt. For a moment, he'd watch her pale skin redden. Then, fearful that he might scorch her, he'd dash to open the door.

After a week of this, unsure of how to share his worries with the girl, Mendel at last called on Lev the butcher to ask if he'd ever heard of people producing heat without fire. Married three times with twelve children, Lev was said to know human nature practically as well as animal slaughter. He was wise to all affairs, privy to every rumor. Without waiting for Mendel to speak, Lev asked him where he'd got his girl.

— She's a cousin, from the big city. She needed a place to stay.

— You have no uncles, Mendel. You have no aunts.

— I guess that means she's an orphan?

— Tell me the truth.

— A week ago, I found her in the corner of my shop, Lev. She asked for work.

— She must have come from somewhere. A girl doesn't just appear.

— She mentioned demons.

— This could be serious. I'd better see her for myself.

Lev thrust his cleaver into the chopping block between them and unhitched his apron. A full head taller than Mendel, and a shoulder broader, he walked at twice the blacksmith's gait. His questions were as rapid as his step. He found out everything that had happened in the previous week—all about her cooking and cleaning and mending and sweeping—by the time they arrived at Mendel's shop. Opening his door, Mendel called out Beitzel's name. No one answered him.

The place appeared deserted. Lev pressed ahead. He looked under the anvil and inside the furnace. He pressed down on the bellows. In the dust that rose, he heard a small sneeze. Lev raised his head. He saw a bony little girl folded up in the rafters.

Beitzel's eyes were dilated with fear. She clung to the beams with fingers and toes to steady her quivering body. Before the butcher could reach up and grab the creature, Mendel began talking to her. He reminded her that Lev was his closest friend, explained that he'd simply wanted to meet her. She retorted that the man looked more likely to slay her.

— That's just the blood on his hands. I've told you that he's a butcher.

— I watched him coming. He was in a hurry to get at me.

— What could he have against someone he's never met?

— Folks have everything against strangers.

— I don't, Beitzel.

— You're different. You believe what I tell you. I trust you.

— Then how could I let someone hurt you?

Yod-Beit glanced down at Lev, big enough to overcome the blacksmith's best intentions and still have strength to eviscerate her. She sighed, and, lowering one limb at a time, settled into Mendel's arms.

Lev made no move. Whatever Beitzel was, he was too stunned to judge. None of his wives, even his first, would have shown the faith in him that this girl had in his friend. Feet on the floor, Beitzel came closer. She curtsied, and, gathering her hempen frock as if it were a silken gown, asked if he'd forgive her impertinence and stay for supper.

When Lev saw Hirsh the cartwright and Zvi the chandler the following morning, he tried to tell them about the meal, but he could scarcely describe why it had been so fine. Beitzel had served a stew of—as best he could tell—Mendel's old trousers boiled in a broth of dirt. Lev had been unable to swallow a single spoonful until he saw what satisfaction Mendel gave the girl by finishing an entire bowl. The butcher had then taken another taste, less wary than the first, and found it, somehow, almost palatable. He'd taken sip after sip as Beitzel asked him about each of his dozen children.

Lev had never heard such curious questions. She hadn't asked names or ages, but had wanted to know how high they could climb and what they thought of heaven, and asked if he could love a boy or girl who didn't sing well. She'd been so pleased to hear that he was fond of all his children, regardless of vocal talent, that she offered him a second serving of stew, which he'd been unable to refuse. Lev had to confess to Zvi and Hirsh that he was as mystified by her queries as by her cooking. He wasn't sure what those demon abductors had done to her poor head before she'd fled their foul swampland, but declared that it no longer mattered. Kindly Mendel had taken her in, and now she was one of them.

Hirsh visited the following day, pretending to meet

Mendel on business. While they discussed hypothetical iron fittings for an imaginary wooden carriage, conjuring intricate plans with elaborate gestures in the air, Beitzel swept dust in circles around them on the floor. Zvi arrived, startled to find Hirsh already there, but the imaginary carriage needed fanciful candles to light the way through the figment of night, so he stepped into the circle swept by Beitzel's broom and entered into their conjecture. The phantom coach grew large enough to convey villages, swift enough to cross continents, driven by the momentum of their scheming, carrying their conversation farther and farther away from the subject all of them wished to discuss.

At last Beitzel set down her broom and said that she couldn't understand why they needed a carriage in the first place. *Your coach may be big and fast. But why would people ever want to leave here?*

None of them had an answer, of course, since, among the three, they'd never ventured more than a mile outside the town gates. So they began to tell her what they believed lay beyond. Zvi envisioned lands that saw neither darkness nor gloom, villages of wax across which grew wick as profuse as flax, blooming blue flame under the setting sun. Not to be outshone, Hirsh described whole countries built of castle brick, turrets turning like gears, slowly rotating stone-wheeled chambers so that folks could all be neighbors one day of the year.

Beitzel did not laugh at them. She simply smiled and said that such places could not compare to the town where they already were.

— How can that be? This is just a poor little village, a place that nobody notices.

— You don't notice it because this village is your home.

— What do you mean?

— I mean that this wouldn't be home to you if you found it exotic. Any place I've ever gone, I haven't belonged.

— But if what you say about our village is true, then you must be at home here, too.

Yod-Beit couldn't dispute them, and that was a problem, as only days remained before the new moon, the night that the town would be rampaged by demons. She looked at Zvi and Hirsh and saw them already flayed. And her Mendel? Even when she shut her eyes, she could hear his bones being crushed on his anvil.

She must have fainted then. Opening her eyes, she found many people gathered around her. She saw Zvi and Hirsh, still in their skin, and Lev, very much alive, with wife and twelve children. There were others as well, come from shop and hovel to meet Mendel's new girl. They brought her sweetmeats. They praised her housekeeping. They called her an angel and begged her to stay with them always.

Each promise she made, as afternoon drew into evening, gripped her more firmly. At last Mendel, barely audible, asked for a marriage vow. Beitzel opened her mouth, but could hear no sound.

It was morning and Beitzel was in bed. She could not figure out how she'd gotten there, nor for how long Mendel had been stroking her hair. Turning to him, she asked if they were married. He sighed, and shook his head.

— You collapsed. I sent everybody home.

— Good. I can't ever be your bride.

— Because I'm a failure?

— No, Mendel. Because I'm a fallen angel.

— Why does that matter, Beitzel? I honestly don't mind your cooking and mending.

— I'm a demon, Mendel. Don't you understand? I'm here to betray you, and everybody else in this village.

— Will you?

— No.

— Why not?

She gazed at him until he saw. He wiped a tear from Beitzel's cheek, not knowing whether it was hers or his own.

— Tomorrow night is the new moon. For you to survive, I have to be gone by then.

— But if you truly . . .

She hushed him with another glance, and then told him the demons' diabolical plan: Heavily cloaked, Boaz would approach the town gate shortly after nightfall. To the first person who saw him, he'd say that he was Beitzel's cousin. The moment the gate was opened to admit him, demons hidden behind every tree and rock would rush in, overpowering the town, and Beitzel couldn't describe what would happen then for fear that, somewhere in the heavens, her words might be mistaken for premonition.

— If I run away tonight, though, you can warn folks here tomorrow. Tell them you made me talk, and chased me out of town. You'll be a hero.

— If you leave, I'll go with you.

— You've never been without a community.

— You'd be my home.

— I'd be your widow.

— Then we'll stay here. We'll let everyone know what you've told me about your cousins.

— They're humans, though. If they find out that I'm a fallen angel . . .

— What's the difference?

— Mendel, humans and demons are enemies. They believe that they're opposites—good versus evil—but their hate is the same.

— And us, Beitzel?

— Together, we're loathsome to everyone.

. . .

Later that day, a bell was rung in the town square. Standing side by side, Beitzel and Mendel waited for everyone to assemble around them in a large circle. Folks waved to the young couple, and one of Lev's girls handed Beitzel, dressed as usual in her plain hempen frock, a daffodil bouquet.

Mendel had never spoken in public. He knew neither stage fright nor show business. He talked as he would to a friend in the street. He said that the following evening folks should expect a plague of demons. In the back they couldn't hear him, and in the front they didn't understand: Just what sort of perverse wedding announcement was the blacksmith making?

Yod-Beit explained. While she'd never addressed a crowd either, the voice lessons she'd received in heaven had taught her to project. She pitched every damning detail. *How do you know?* asked Hirsh. *She's a demon,* shouted everybody else. She nodded. The circle imploded.

Mendel begged people to be gentle with his Beitzel. He pleaded that she wasn't a real devil, grotesque and perverse, just a poor angel who'd happened somehow to lose her balance. They dragged her down the stone steps beneath the bell tower, shedding daffodils, to the village's solitary prison cell.

Forged by Mendel's grandfather, the cell had scarcely been used, except as an underground aviary for the night watchman Ariel's owls. The owls were roused by the ruckus. As the door was thrust open, they flew away, and Beitzel was thrown in their place. *Traitress,* folks shouted. *You can't scare us, demon-girl. Let the devils attack today or next year. If they try, we'll crucify their little moll.*

Mendel pressed through the mob. In front of the iron cage, he faced Hirsh and Zvi and Lev, and, behind them, everyone else he'd ever known. Unable to follow the logic of punishing someone for being honest, he asked why he wasn't locked away as well.

— You're innocent, Mendel.

— Then let me in the cell. It's prison for me to stand here with you, barred from my Beitzel.

For an instant, the mob quivered with confusion. Then, collective muscle flexed, the crowd pounded him into the dungeon.

Ariel the watchman was lonesome without his owls. His wife slept at night while he worked, and neither had seen the other awake in all their married years. While that was the basis of their famed connubial bliss—how they remained, so to speak, the lovers of each other's dreams—both had to seek elsewhere for companionship. His wife had her affairs, and Ariel had his aviary.

The owls had not only been pets for the watchman. Year by year, he'd gone blind overlooking his wife's liaisons. The owls were his eyes. On the night he was abandoned by them, he stood at the town gate beneath the new moon, not knowing where the night ended and where his gloom began.

He talked to himself as he'd spoken to his owls. *The winds are mighty strong,* he said.

Punishing weather, a voice responded.

— Who's there? It's past curfew.

— My name is Boaz. I'm Beitzel's cousin. I have to see her. Please let me in?

— Beitzel is in jail.

— In jail? What happened?

Ariel didn't know the circumstances of Beitzel's incarceration. Each villager had left to others the task of informing him, as nobody wanted to take responsibility for the loss of his birds.

— Aren't you curious, Ariel?

— Yes.

— I'll stand guard for you while you find out. Just leave those keys here with me.

As Ariel reached out to hand him the ring, the winds turned. Talons drawn, an owl plunged between them, catching Boaz by the snout and ripping him away from the gate. The demon's horrible bellow gelded the watchman's ears. And stirred a hundred more devils, who charged the town as the owl hauled Boaz toward the end of the world.

The furor awoke the entire village. Folks opened their doors, and peered out into the night. They asked one another what was happening, and remembered Beitzel's warning.

Lacking armaments, they grabbed as weaponry the cookware and cutlery that Mendel had forged them, and scrambled toward the town square. Ariel was already there, blindly stumbling over the cobblestones, deafly stuttering the word *owl* over and over again.

People looked up. The whole sky was alive. A thousand owls soared over their village, flying as if feathers of a single wing, so tight was their formation. The wing dipped as demons hammered at the walls of their town, swiping up the villains with a hundred honed talons.

Of course the shrewdness of owls was well known to the townsfolk: Because owls' eyes are fixed open, even as they sleep, and their hearing penetrates all that they cannot see, the species has accumulated vast wisdom over the generations, an inheritance the envy of humans. Here Ariel's flock had heard the truth in Beitzel's tale and raised a squadron, while the villagers had denounced her and sent her to prison. Whose fault had it been? Who was to blame? They quibbled until dawn. Nobody saw the owls scatter, and it was blind Ariel who first remarked that the sun seemed not to be rising, but dropping straight down on them.

Folding back great wings of flame, an angel emerged from the light. He was more massive than any man the villagers had ever seen, yet as unblemished as a newborn. People shuffled to their feet to greet the distinguished visitor, trying frantically to get rid of their useless cookware by passing it back and forth. Ignoring their fulsome greetings, the angel said in a voice that rang like a towering bronze bell above their heads, *Where is Yod-Beit?*

The villagers looked at one another. They asked, a bit nervously, if he meant Beitzel.

— Where is Yod-Beit, the fallen angel, who betrayed her fellow demons to save your lives? For this great deed, she has been recalled to heaven.

— *That* Yod-Beit? She may be under the bell tower, resting.

— Bring her to me.

Lev led a delegation down to the dungeon. They found Beitzel and Mendel asleep on the stone floor, curled up in the cradle of each other's arms. Lev unlocked the cell door. Zvi crouched down and rocked the couple awake. As Beitzel opened her eyes, he told her that there was an angel waiting outside for her.

— What does he want?

— He's come to take you back to heaven.

— Send him away.

— Don't be afraid. Up above, they saw what you did for us, in spite of us. You deserve this.

— No, I don't. You've never been in heaven. Do you know why I was banished?

She stood up. Mendel rose with her. The men looked at him. He didn't have the answer. He hadn't thought to ask her.

— I was cast out of heaven because I couldn't sing on key.

— That can't be.

— I wasn't the only one. There were nine others the same night. Nine other young seraphim, just like me.

— What happened to them?

— They burned on the way down. *Shooting stars,* you call them here, tormenting them with your petty wishes as they fry.

— Singing off-key can't be the only reason for banishment.

— You're right. Some angels are tossed out because they're too short or fat. My cousin Boaz was ousted because he had flat feet. Folks believe that heaven is special. It could be as good and bad as any other place. What makes it so much worse is that it tries to be perfect.

— You're sure of this?

— I won't go back. My home is here with Mendel. I won't be a devil or an angel. It's enough to be his Beitzel.

Yod-Beit took Mendel's hand, and sent the delegation to tell the heavenly messenger her decision.

The angel scarcely waited for Lev to stammer Beitzel's refusal. (*A most generous offer . . . Regretfully has prior commitments . . . So grateful that you thought of her . . .*) Wordlessly turning his back on the village, the messenger opened his wings to the sun, and faded into its distant glow.

Folks started to gather their cookware. They didn't talk or even look at one another, yet none of them went home. Nobody left the square. As minutes gave way to hours, people glanced up at the sky less often. They milled about, walking off expectation, letting go the notion that heaven, rejected by feisty Beitzel, might come back for them instead.

Of course heaven had no such intentions. Returning from the world without Yod-Beit, her guardian found the gathered seraphim fuming. *Consider what it means for celestial prestige,* they said, *to be snubbed by a fallen angel in front of those earthly vermin.* He nodded, afraid that if he tried to speak, his voice would tremble like a crystal serving bell. They demanded that he return to her. They decreed that her apotheosis was not an offer, but an order.

He descended again with a train of deputies. The flight was always trying, for the wings they wore were borrowed beams of sunlight insulated with golden fleece that would ignite at the slightest fall from grace. Moreover, people no longer saw their lofty appearance as any great miracle, but, especially in big cities, expected aerobatic feats. Villagers were less demanding, since the angels didn't have to compete with professional entertainers—circus trapezists and tightrope walkers—yet when a mission was significant enough to call for a conclave of them, they were expected at least to fly in formation, heralding their visitation.

That got people's attention. The villagers dropped their pots and pans. They raised heads and hands, as if expecting a gift. Instead they got an ultimatum.

A crowd of them went to Beitzel, to communicate the angels' demand. Everyone followed as she mounted the dungeon stairs into daylight. They watched her stride across the village square, to the cluster of angels. She approached them as an equal. Folks marveled that her height did not recede with distance. By the time she reached the heavenly coven, little Beitzel appeared as large as her persecutors. They cowered as she spoke. They clung to their wings of fire. None of the townsfolk could hear what she said to her fellow celestials, but when she turned her back on them, the angels looked broken.

With effort, they levitated. One slipped and immolated. The remainder scattered, scarcely visible on the horizon as Beitzel met Mendel in the middle of the square. She took his hands, and gazed at him, as little and fragile as she'd ever been.

— Heaven isn't done.

— The angels are all gone. It doesn't look like they'll be back again.

— I know, Mendel. But this evening a celestial storm will come and take me away. Heaven will claim me by force.

Mendel tried to comfort her. He proposed that she wait out the storm in the cell beneath the bell tower. She pronounced that it would collapse. He offered to forge her armor of iron that no wind could lift. She foretold that it would corrode to dust. She would not be consoled. She dismissed all ordinary precautions. As the clouds came, she declared that she'd have to face the storm. As the thunder rolled, she confessed that she couldn't withstand the tempest alone.

People scrambled for cover. Mendel didn't budge. He wrapped his arms around Beitzel's shoulders. He vowed that if heaven wanted Yod-Beit, it would have to take them together.

Of course the celestial sphere was too high a climb for the haughtiest kings, let alone a grimy blacksmith. The winds rose to meet his affront. A hurricane wrapped around the couple, quickening to rip them apart. Clothing was stripped away, shredded. They clung to each other's skin. They pressed so close that the air could no longer distinguish between them, and could only batter them together. Thrown off their feet, they were thrust onto the ground. With a jolt, the last barrier between them broke. Heaven and earth mingled inside the couple.

All at once the winds dropped. The lightning thundered off. The clouds slouched away under their dark shrouds of rain. Folks crept out of their houses to see if Beitzel and Mendel had survived, could be revived. They found the couple still writhing, oblivious that the storm had passed.

For nine full months, Yod-Beit's belly swelled. Every day folks fretted over whether her naked rebellion with Mendel would beget a plague or just a lump of coal. The blacksmith was angered by neighbors' slights, which he couldn't quite refute. Beitzel simply smiled.

And then one morning, when the sky was as blue as a heavenly reflecting pool, Yod-Beit, fallen angel, delivered her husband an ordinary baby girl.

EDITORS' AFTERWORD

Professor Jay Katz vanished on February 9, 2008, the day that he submitted these twelve tales for publication. On that date, he also sent a letter of resignation to his university, instructing the dean to disperse his books and incinerate his papers. Since then, there have been countless reports in the media, often spectacular, about the professor's disappearance. As his editors, we feel obliged to attempt, as best we can, to set the record straight.

The first public report that Professor Katz was missing attracted little notice. A brief wire item appeared on February 23, after repeated inquiries by his university failed to locate him in Europe. While the article didn't mention the professor's extracurricular work on the Lamedh-Vov, a notoriously radical Hasidic rabbi named Binyamin Krupnik issued a statement the following day claiming that Jay Katz had been struck from this world as punishment by God. Purporting to speak on Yahweh's behalf, the rebbe accused the scholar of betraying a sacred trust, incurring the heavenly retribution that his unholy activities deserved. Krupnik was then in hiding, wanted by Interpol for several kidnappings, so his statement put Katz's disappearance on the evening news. That's when we came forward, offering to share our author's manuscript with select reporters, hoping to help in the search effort.

We would like to emphasize that we didn't intend to abet Rabbi Krupnik by giving credence to his outlandish indictment, but neither were we trying—as others have suggested—to implicate him in our author's disappearance. That accusation was made by Krupnik's religious enemies, led by the reform rabbi Omri Zvi, who charged that Krupnik's sect was threatened by what Jay Katz had learned. According to Zvi's reasoning, a Lamedh-Vov comprised of gamblers and whores, let alone fallen angels, would make a mockery of orthodox dogma, undermining the political power of the religious parties in Israel. In other words, Krupnik was the one who'd banished Professor Katz from this world—by having him assassinated and laying blame on God. There was no more evidence of this than of Krupnik's exalted claims, but the potential of murder, the prospect of martyrdom, made the story irresistible to talk shows and tabloids. Jay Katz's destiny was out of our hands.

And then came the inevitable backlash, the denunciation of Professor Katz by secular critics, who called his tales fraudulent, saying that the cause of his disappearance was suicide: Jay Katz had made up his story about Yaakov ben Eleazer's list of thirty-six, fabricating the tales in an attempt to revive a career gone stagnant, only to be overcome by guilt after he submitted the phony manuscript. First he'd resigned, and then he'd drowned himself. With each telling, the story was more elaborate. He'd heaved himself from a cliff. He'd thrown himself to the sharks. Several prominent academics, whose names we will not mention, began circulating a petition urging us not to publish this book. We have categorically refused—and been slandered on dozens of blogs as the real cause of his demise.

The fate of Jay Katz has now become fodder for conspiracy theories too muddled to describe. We would like to respond by referring readers to the professor's own Foreword, in which he asserts his intention to continue pursuing stories of the Lamedh-Vov. *Do not seek me,* he writes. *I cannot say if I'll ever return.* We would like to propose that the most likely answer to the enigma, more probable than divine retribution or political assassination or even professional suicide, is that Jay Katz is unobtrusively doing his work, quietly following the course set by Yaakov's list. We are aware that his brief media celebrity, though now passed, would make this difficult, that a whole year without a single sighting would be highly unlikely. Yet there is another circumstance, which has not previously been disclosed in print, that may account for his preternatural stealth, if not explain it.

The university did not incinerate Jay Katz's papers after he vanished, as he requested, yet all forty-three boxes are now missing from the underground warehouse. His academic records are also gone from the registrar's office, though investigators have found no tampering with the locked file cabinets. Stranger, nobody who corresponded with him over the years has been able to find his old letters in their archives. Even the few pictures of him that have been published on book jackets and in newspapers seem blurrier than people remember, inexplicably vague. It's as if some vast act of erasure were taking place, leaving behind only his accounts of Alef the Idiot and Chet the Cheat and Yod the Inhuman for people to contemplate. We are by no means a religious press, yet some of us have begun to wonder whether Jay Katz is being protected in some supernal way, hidden for the sake of his work, carried to the brink of anonymity lest anybody try to pursue him, or threaten his calling by regarding him as a ———

But such matters are beyond us. The Lamedh-Vov belong to another realm. We will not question what cannot be known.

—THE EDITORS

ACKNOWLEDGMENTS

The author gratefully acknowledges the support of the Mac-Dowell Colony, the MacNamara Foundation, the Ucross Foundation, and the Corporation of Yaddo, as well as Modernism Gallery and the Judah L. Magnes Museum.

ABOUT THE AUTHOR

JONATHON KEATS is an artist, novelist, essayist, and journalist. He is the author of the novel *The Pathology of Lies*. He is also the art critic for *San Francisco* magazine, a columnist for *Wired* magazine and *Artweek*, a correspondent for *Art & Antiques*, and a contributor to publications including *The Washington Post, The Boston Globe, Popular Science, Prospect, Forbes Life, Art & Auction*, and Salon.com. Keats has been awarded fellowships by Yaddo, the MacDowell Colony, the Ucross Foundation, the MacNamara Foundation, and the Poetry Center at the University of Arizona, and has chaired the National Book Critics Circle fiction award committee. He lives in San Francisco.